The Right Time

Book 4 of the *Love Unexpected* series

Delaney Diamond

Chapter One

Ransom Stewart didn't move fast enough.

The green drink landed in his face and splashed down the front of his Armani suit, dousing the white shirt, striped tie, and the undershirt. Conversation in the restaurant screeched to a halt amid surprised gasps and startled glances.

Using a cloth napkin, he wiped away the apple martini dripping down his face and mopped the excess from the damp hair hanging across his brow.

"You're a shitty person. You want a break?" Lisa hissed at him, green eyes flashing with anger and hurt. "Let's take a break. How about we make it permanent?" She shoved back the chair with such force it toppled with a crash behind her. She snatched her purse from the table, and after one last death glare, marched away. Brunette hair swinging across her back, she stalked out of the restaurant with her head held high.

So much for going to a public place to have "the

talk."

With a heavy sigh, Ransom walked around the table, picked up the chair, and returned to his seat.

He'd been wanting to have this conversation with Lisa for some time, ever since she started talking about babies and marriage. When they initially met two years ago, she'd been just as goal-oriented as he, but over the past few months a change occurred. Words like *biological clock* crept into their conversations more frequently, and she made a point of mentioning which of her friends got engaged or married.

He enjoyed her company when she came to Chicago from her home base in New York, but the strength of their relationship rested on the beauty of living in different cities, where they could go about their own lives however they wanted. As an attorney, he worked eighty-plus hours a week, per the norm. She herself, as a principal in a consulting firm, worked long hours as well. Lately, though, her visits had become more frequent, just like talk of marriage and clocks.

The final straw came a few weeks ago when she visited and mentioned the possibility of moving to Chicago. That's when he recognized the situation had gotten out of hand.

He'd brought her to one of the best restaurants in the city to let her down easy, and hopefully save himself the drama that he expected to come. Unfortunately, the drama played out in public, rather than private. A miscalculation on his part.

The waitress came over, a twenty-something-year-old dressed in a white shirt and black slacks, hair pulled back into a single long braid. She cleared her throat. "Are you all right, sir?"

"Yes, I'm fine." Ransom dabbed the stained shirt with a napkin. Hopefully it wasn't ruined.

"I could get you some club soda to help with that." The waitress clasped her hands in front of her, appearing at a loss at how to handle the situation.

Ransom smiled to put her at ease. "Thanks. You can remove my date's plate, bring the check when you have a chance, and a refill on the wine, please."

Lucky for him, the tossed drink missed his meal of prime rib, scalloped potatoes, and bacon-wrapped asparagus. Only a few drops had landed on the edge of the white plate, which he swiped off with the napkin. He picked up his fork and knife and cut into the meat. No point in letting a perfectly cooked prime rib go to waste, particularly one as tender and costly as this one.

"Yes, sir." The waitress nodded and deftly lifted Lisa's plate and empty glass from the other side of the table. The hum of restaurant conversation restarted.

Ransom could be embarrassed about the way the night had ended, but he'd been called names before, and this wasn't the first time he'd had a blowup in a public place. Though it was certainly the wettest.

He finished his meal with the extra glass of wine, occasionally checking stock quotes and email on his phone. He returned a few messages and made a note to himself about a case he was working on. All in all, the evening had turned out to be productive, despite the disastrous encounter with Lisa.

Later, he stepped out into the night and buttoned his jacket. The noise of the city surrounded him—cars going by and the sound of a siren tearing through the night air. More than ever, he looked forward to his trip in a few days. His coworkers, Giles and

Stephanie, were getting married in the Bahamas, and the time off in a warmer climate would be a welcome change of pace.

He didn't usually do vacations. A day or two here and there was all he could manage. His hectic schedule simply didn't allow the luxury of downtime, but he had scheduled an extra day at the beginning of the trip to relax on the beach and work on a tan. One day of relaxation wouldn't hurt.

Ransom handed the valet the numbered card to retrieve his car, and soon the metallic-gray Porsche Cayenne eased up to the front door. After handing the young man a hefty tip, he hopped in and took off toward his condo in the Loop, Chicago's business district.

Since he had the rest of his Saturday night free, he might as well get some work done. He pressed the recorder on his phone. "Prepare summary judgment for the Standcomp case." Ransom pressed *End* and saved the reminder.

Thinking about Lisa as he cruised down the highway, he sighed. The timing was all wrong for them to move into a more permanent relationship, but it was hard to explain that to her.

Having her move to Chicago would be distracting, and so would having them move into a more permanent relationship, such as marriage. He envisioned them as a power couple—both ambitious and successful—and knew they could be really good together…eventually. But she wanted to move too fast. He still hadn't made partner, a goal he saw within reach—this year, for sure.

Besides, he was only thirty-seven. He had his whole life ahead of him. He simply wasn't ready to settle down yet.

Ransom eased his vehicle into the underground parking garage of his building. No point in crying over spilled milk. He had work to do. He took the elevator up to his condo and within minutes, he was in his home office, hard at work.

****

Days like this made it hard for Sophie Bradshaw to remember why she'd enjoyed being a flight attendant for nine years, despite meeting crappy passengers like the man in 2B.

Matthias Ditka thought the entire crew was there to do his bidding. Each time he asked for a refill of vodka, he yelled the request and rudely yanked the small bottle from their hands with an ungracious utterance of "About time." The obnoxious behavior only increased with the length of the flight.

Sophie groaned when the call light came on again. "What does he want now?" she grumbled.

He'd managed to spoil her anticipation of the trip to the Bahamas, an arrangement she'd maneuvered by calling in a favor to swap routes with another flight attendant.

"Probably wants us to rub his feet." Jalinda, one of the other flight attendants, rolled her eyes.

This was Sophie's first time working with Jalinda, but she liked her a lot. Their similar temperament and the other woman's sense of humor made the trip much more enjoyable.

"You take him this time, or I may end up punching him in the face," Jalinda added.

Sophie laughed out loud and slammed a hand over

her mouth. "I would love to see that."

Taking a deep breath, she squared her shoulders and walked down the first-class aisle. She stopped at the seat where a burly bearded man sat holding an empty mini vodka bottle.

"I need another one of these, pronto," he said, way too loud.

Sophie leaned forward and spoke quietly. "I'm sorry, sir, but I'm going to have to cut you off."

"Cut me off?" he bellowed, causing heads to turn and Sophie to wince. "This is first class."

"I understand. However, we can't simply—"

He grabbed her hand and yanked her forward. The fingers around her wrist tightened so much, pain shot up her arm. "Listen here, missy. Either you or the other waitress can bring me something else to drink. I don't care who does it. Do it now, or I'll go back there and get the drink myself."

His breath reeked of the liquor he'd consumed since takeoff, and she suspected he'd been drinking before then.

"You're hurting me. Let go." Sophie fisted her right hand, prepared to land a solid punch across the side of the man's face if he didn't release her by the time she counted to five in her head.

One.

"Are you going to do as I ask? I am a customer and paid a small fortune for this damn seat."

"Please let go of my arm."

Two.

"I'll let go when you give me the answer I want."

Three.

"Let her go."

The low tenor came from a few feet in front of

her. Sophie had been completely oblivious to anyone moving toward them, and her gaze collided with that of a tall male, the hottie from a few rows back. His large frame dominated the aisle.

He smelled inviting. She detected a fresh, almost minty fragrance coming from him, and he looked like he'd just stepped out of the pages of *GQ*, with a clean-shaven face, thick, dark hair neatly combed back from his face, and a powder-blue shirt that clung to his trim physique. A navy tie, black trousers, and black oxfords completed the look.

Despite his civilized appearance, he exuded an underlying roughness as he glared down at the grip the passenger had on her wrist, his body obviously tensed, jaw set in an inflexible line.

"Who's going to make me let her go?" Matthias stared up at the younger man.

Thick, dark eyebrows snapped together. "I am. Believe me, I'm itching to let off some steam, and it would give me great pleasure to use you to do it."

Matthias quickly dropped Sophie's hand, and she gladly stepped back from him, rubbing her wrist.

"Are you okay?" The man searched her face.

He had nice lips. She seldom noticed a man's lips, but his were thin with an appealing curve. Then there were his striking blue eyes, bright and clear, almost see-through, like glass. An empty hole in his right earlobe suggested he wore an earring, which was interestingly incongruous with his otherwise preppy appearance.

She nodded. "I'm fine, thank you."

"I just want another drink. Is that so wrong?" the irate passenger hollered.

"She said she was cutting you off, and from the

looks of it, you definitely don't need anything else to drink."

"Who are you, her daddy?" the wider man growled.

Her savior bent at the waist, getting right in the face of the burly passenger, and said, "I'm the guy who's going to stuff that empty bottle up your ass."

"Thank you so much, sir," Sophie interrupted quickly. While she appreciated the assistance, the last thing she wanted was an incident on the plane. Despite her desire to punch the prick in the face herself, flight attendants must maintain their cool at all times.

She placed a restraining hand on her savior's shoulder. His hard, muscular shoulder. Tempted to rub her palm up and down his arm, she snatched away her hand. "I can take it from here."

He straightened, and the way his gaze traveled over her face sent her pulse beating faster and out of control. This man rattled her.

"Thank you," she said, settling into a cool, professional voice. She fixed a smile on her face. "Please have a seat."

He didn't move, his body still taut, as if ready to spring into action at her command. His gaze lingered on her a little longer, dragging from her eyes down the vest and skirt of her cranberry uniform. She straightened her back, skin tingling under the blatant inspection.

Then she saw it—a softening of his features. Interest. He blinked. Mutual attraction shimmered on the air between them. Then he leaned closer, and her body tensed, tightening like the string pulled taut on a bow.

"He shouldn't have put his hands on you."

His breath hit the corner of her mouth, and he held her gaze to punctuate the statement. Neither moved. Time halted.

Then, as if none of that had happened, he turned and walked the few rows back to his seat. Sophie let the trapped air out of her lungs, releasing the tension from her shoulders and back.

A round of applause went up through the cabin, and Matthias's face flushed a bright shade of crimson. Sophie smiled reassuringly to the applauding passengers and then walked briskly toward the galley.

"What happened?" Jalinda asked, filling a glass with ice to complete another drink request.

Sophie rubbed her red wrist. "Mr. Dickhead grabbed me."

Jalinda's eyes widened. "What? You need to write that up."

Protocol dictated that any disturbance had to be written up and reported.

"I will."

"Are you all right?"

"I'm fine. 5A came over and stopped him."

Jalinda shot a look around the dividing wall and then wiggled her brows at Sophie. "Oh yes, I remember him when he came on board. He is *hot.*"

"I guess," Sophie said, pretending to be uninterested.

"What are you, blind?"

"He's all right."

"Oh, come on. He is H-O-T."

"Don't you have a passenger to take care of?" Sophie asked.

Jalinda rolled her eyes and went to deliver the

drink.

As soon as her back was turned, Sophie checked the passenger manifest and saw the name of the passenger who'd come to her aid.

Ransom Stewart.

An unusual, but strong name. Brash. Commanding. Just like him.

Peeking around the dividing wall, she took another look at Ransom. He seemed absorbed in whatever he was writing, head bent over a spiral-bound notebook, brow furrowed as he concentrated. He'd been writing since he came on the flight.

Idly, she wondered what he did for a living. Something corporate, like banking. Of that she was certain.

Jalinda started down the aisle and Sophie hurriedly replaced the manifest and began prepping for the lunch service.

She had work to do. Enough drooling over a man she'd never see again.

Chapter Two

Ransom hated wasting time. Even if that time was spent on Paradise Island in the beautiful Bahamas. There were a dozen other things he could be doing instead of standing around, sipping champagne during a wedding reception at the Atlantis Resort. After spending yesterday in relaxation mode, he needed to focus again. He had interrogatories to read, briefs to write, and client files to review.

The wedding had taken place over an hour before on a green lawn overlooking the blue Bahamian waters. At the moment, Ransom stood with the groom, Giles, at the U-shaped bar where bartenders filled drink orders for family, friends, and coworkers from the law firm.

Giles was a lanky corporate attorney a few inches taller than Ransom, with dirty-blond hair and a gregarious personality more befitting someone in sales than law. His smiling face camouflaged a sharp mind and made opponents settle into a false sense of security so that he was often able to outmaneuver opposing counsel.

"She threw the whole drink in your face?" Giles asked.

Ransom had just recounted his experience with Lisa.

"The entire glass."

Giles chuckled. "I'm so sorry to hear that."

"You look really sorry," Ransom said dryly, taking a sip of his martini. One day he'd probably laugh at the story, too, but for the moment couldn't find the humor in being punished for his honesty. "I've barely seen you drink anything all night. It's your wedding day. Drink up."

"No, thanks. I need to stay sober for later."

"Not as if you two haven't slept together before," Ransom said.

"But this will be the first time we've slept together as husband and wife."

The road to getting to this point had been rocky. Stephanie almost marrying another man had catapulted Giles into action to win back the woman he loved. Tears had filled his friend's eyes when he saw Stephanie walk down the aisle, and even now, every so often his eyes found her wherever she was in the room and lingered there. Softening. As if he couldn't believe his good fortune.

Both men walked away from the bar and stood against the wall, watching the festivities. The musicians had been playing a blend of rock, pop, and soul. Right now the lead singer crooned into the microphone, her voice dripping with a slower, sexier version of James Brown's "Hot Pants," with her gyrations bordering on too lewd for a wedding.

"Heard anything about the invitations yet?" Ransom asked.

As was the custom, invitations for the partners' annual cocktail party would be going out soon. The event rotated to the four cities in which the firm had an office, and this year it would take place in Atlanta.

"Nah. I'm not worried about it."

Ransom's head swung toward his friend. "How could you not be worried?"

"I know it's too soon for me to get an invite. You should be getting yours soon, though."

"I hope."

"You will." There was a pause. "Becoming a partner is all you care about, isn't it?" Giles asked.

"In all the time you've known me, what else have you ever heard me talk about?"

Ransom had been working toward an equity partnership ever since he left a big law practice eight years ago to join Abraham, MacKenzie & Wong. With other offices in Atlanta, Los Angeles, and New York, the midsized firm was known for rewarding its attorneys with excellent bonuses and opportunities for advancement.

Giles was quiet for a while. Then he spoke in a voice weighted with thoughts. "I used to want the same thing, but now I'm not so sure."

The words hit Ransom like a blow to the chest, so foreign he almost gasped. "Are you saying you don't want to be a partner?"

"I'm not saying that. I want it, but it's no longer as important as I thought it would be. I'm not going to lecture you. You know what you want, but I can't help thinking about me and Stephanie. I almost lost her to another man because I didn't realize what a good woman I had, too consumed with pursuing the brass ring. When in reality, she is the brass ring—hell, the gold ring. I'm telling you, man, once you fall in love, everything else becomes so…irrelevant."

Ransom took a sip of his martini. "I don't plan on falling in love."

"No one ever plans on falling in love."

Ransom groaned. "Please don't tell me how great it is to be married when you've been married less than a day."

Giles chuckled. "I wouldn't dream of it. I'm new at this, but it does feel great."

"I'll see how great you think marriage is in a couple of years. I've been in serious relationships before, and they consume too much of my time. I have a new motto. No commitments. No girlfriends. I need to stay focused." The debacle with Lisa had taught him that much. Timing was everything, and right now he should concentrate on his career. A committed relationship could come later, when he had the time to devote to it.

"I understand what you're saying. But believe me, there's never going to be a right time to make a commitment. There will always be something else that comes up. You just have to seize the moment."

Ransom shot him a sideways glance. "You are so whipped."

Giles chuckled, his eyes sparkling with amusement despite the dig. "And I couldn't be happier."

"Or luckier. I don't know what you said to get Stephanie to break her engagement with Alexander, but it worked."

"Yeah, I know I'm lucky." Giles looked extremely grateful, a smile of tenderness on his face as he gazed across the room at his new bride.

Stephanie was in the middle of a conversation with her mother, a tall, elegant-looking black woman with salt-and-pepper hair that curled around her ears and nape. Stephanie's hair was styled into a series of twists atop her head. The long sleeveless gown flattered the lines of her svelte frame. She glanced away from her mother and looked at Giles, and no one could miss the connection between them. The messages their eyes sent to each other were known to them alone.

Stephanie bit her lip and didn't even seem to notice that Ransom stood beside her new husband. When her mother spoke, she returned her attention to her.

"If I hadn't done something completely impulsive, I never would have won Stephanie back and be standing here today. Can't believe I almost lost her for good." Giles shook his head.

"Hmm," Ransom said, for lack of anything better to say. He often found effusive declarations of love and feelings to not only be boring, but exaggerations. He scanned the room, searching for a viable candidate for a hookup later. "There simply aren't enough single women at this wedding."

"My mistake. I should have given more thought to your needs when Stephanie and I put together the guest list."

Ransom drained his glass and set it on a table nearby. "You can work on that for your next wedding."

"Not happening, friend. She's stuck with me for life."

"Unless yours becomes one of the forty to fifty percent of marriages that end in divorce." With numbers like that, he could never understand why couples spent such an exorbitant amount of money celebrating one single day—one single moment—that would soon be forgotten in the monotony, stress, and acrimony of married life.

"You know as well as I do those numbers are questionable, but even if true, it means fifty to sixty percent of them last. And don't worry, I won't tell Stephanie the horrible conversation you've sucked me into on our wedding day."

Ransom grinned. He couldn't dispute the topic wasn't the best. "Please don't. She'd never forgive me."

Giles and Stephanie exchanged another look and his friend shoved away from the wall. "I think it's time I get my bride out of here." He clapped Ransom on the arm. "Maybe Lisa wasn't the right woman for you, but one of these days, you're going to meet her. Seize the moment or you'll end up with regrets." He flashed a grin and then strolled to the other side of the room.

Ransom checked his watch. He could go to his room and work, but it was still early. He scanned the room again. Sleeping with a coworker was out of the question, and the few other single women there didn't pique his interest enough to pursue them. He'd go to the casino and gamble a bit, and then head back to his room to get some work done.

Unlike Giles, Ransom had his priorities straight.

Chapter Three

Ransom sat at the roulette table with a British couple off to his right. They whisper-argued before placing each bet, the female gesticulating wildly, emphasizing the words with her hands, while the male took slow, deep breaths every few seconds and shook his head, then spoke between his teeth. A couple of seats down to the left sat a boisterous American male in a black T-shirt that highlighted his pale skin. He clearly hadn't taken advantage of the sun's rays yet.

Ransom watched the little white ball bounce along the wheel and land on red twenty-one. He grunted, a sound of dismay that joined the groans of loss going up from the table. He'd lost sixty dollars this time. Perhaps roulette wasn't his game.

"Well, if it isn't my hero." The friendly voice came from off to his right.

Ransom looked up to see the flight attendant from Noble Airlines, and his eyes settled on her in appreciation. She wore more makeup than the day before, her lashes brushed into long sweeps over wide gray eyes. The prim and proper uniform had been exchanged for a touristy sunburst sundress that brightened her light, amber-toned skin. Her hair was much longer than he originally realized. On the plane it had been pinned at her nape in a wavy ball, but this evening she let it hang loose to fall over her shoulders and graze the tops of a pair of impressive breasts. Colorful bangles adorned her wrists, and a pair of gold sandals showed off shapely calves.

His spirits immediately lifted, and his interest instantly piqued. "Heroes wear capes," he tossed back.

"Not all heroes," she said, a smile on her face.

He played with the chips in front of him while keeping an eye on her. "I'm pretty sure I saved the passenger. You looked ready to hit him in the face."

She laughed, a sweet, feminine sound that tugged at his gut and made an older man walking by turn to watch her appreciatively before continuing on his way. She didn't seem to notice, keeping her eyes on him.

"I thought about punching him one good time, but then I would have lost my job. So you saved me from making a really bad decision. Anyway, I just wanted to let you know how much I appreciated your help. Thank you."

"You thanked me on the plane," Ransom said.

She shrugged a slender shoulder. "I wanted to do it again."

Ransom was getting some very positive vibes from their interaction. Perhaps he'd get lucky on this trip after all. He waved at the chair beside him. "Have a seat. I need a little lady luck at the tables. I haven't been doing too well."

She didn't hesitate to sit down, confirming his suspicion that she'd been waiting for an invitation to join him. With a cross of her legs, she pulled the hem of the dress down to her knees, but not before he caught a flash of one smooth thigh.

"What's your name?" he asked.

"Sophie."

"I'm Ransom."

"That's a very unusual name." She faced him, one arm resting on the table.

"I get that a lot. My family has this weird tradition of giving all the men in the family first names that begin with the letter R. They were getting close to running out of names when I came along."

She laughed again, and he didn't care if it was fake or genuine. He liked the sound and wouldn't mind hearing it again, and often.

"Do you gamble?" he asked.

"I've played the slots a few times, but never roulette." Her gaze swept the table. "I don't know much about it."

"Apparently neither do I. Which number do you think I should choose?"

Her gray eyes widened. "I have no idea. I don't want that kind of pressure."

"No pressure. Like I said, I haven't had much luck, so you can't possibly make things any worse. Pick a number."

"Hmmm." She tapped her chin, gaze jumping from one number to the next. "How about thirty-three?"

"Thirty-three it is." Ransom placed his chips in the

square.

Sophie gasped. "You're really going to do that?"

Her shock amused him. "Absolutely."

After making a last call for bets, the croupier spun the wheel. The white ball bounced across the numbers and eventually stopped.

"Black, thirty-three," the croupier called.

Sophie's eyes widened and she covered her mouth, muffling a squeal.

"You *are* good luck," Ransom said. He collected his winnings. "Come on, and I'll buy you a drink."

He stood and Sophie joined him.

"I should be buying you a drink. After all, you saved me."

"Enough of that hero nonsense. I'm buying because it's the least I could do for helping me win back some of the money I lost." He also wanted to get her alone to get to know her better.

Ransom cashed in his chips, and they walked through the busy casino toward the bar where they sat on stools at one end. "What would you like to drink?" he asked.

"A white wine spritzer, please."

"A white wine spritzer for the lady, and a rum and Coke for me," he instructed the bartender. Then he gave Sophie his undivided attention. "What made you choose lucky number thirty-three?"

She shrugged. "I didn't know how lucky it would be. I picked that number because tomorrow is my birthday, and I'll be thirty-three."

"Well, happy birthday."

"Thank you." Brilliant teeth flashed in a smile that beamed across her face.

"Are your girlfriends joining you later?"

"No, I'm here by myself."

"No way. What about a boyfriend?" He was on a blatant fishing expedition.

Her smile tightened a little. Interesting.

"He's not here, either."

"Hard to believe."

"Believe it." She shifted on the stool.

Ransom stroked his chin, noting her crestfallen expression. "Trouble in paradise?"

She sighed. "Is it that obvious?"

"The clipped response and your expression gave it away. What happened?"

"He's just...always been an ass, and then he did the most asshole-y thing imaginable."

For a split second, a grimace of pain crossed her features. If he'd glanced away, he would have missed it.

"He cheated on me with the waitress at my favorite vegetarian restaurant. Needless to say, I was devastated and can never go back there again."

"He really is an ass."

"Of course he's been blowing up my phone, calling constantly and saying how sorry he is and how it'll never happen again."

"But you're not falling for it?"

"I..." Her brow wrinkled. "We've been together for a long time, so I'm kinda...torn, I guess. The truth is, he seldom made time for me before, and now the tables have turned. I'm not giving him any of my time. He probably doesn't even remember my birthday is on Sunday."

"Sounds like an inattentive idiot."

"He is. One who only cares about himself and his needs, and never keeps his promises. That's his MO.

Make a promise, break a promise. Anything and everything is much more important than me. Now we can add cheater to his list of flaws." She took a deep breath and pressed a hand to her chest. "I'm so sorry. I didn't mean to go off on a tangent like that."

She blushed, and the pink color brightened her cheeks in a becoming way.

"No need to apologize. Seems like you needed to get that off your chest."

"I guess I did." She absentmindedly rubbed the surface of the bar with the tip of one finger.

"Feel better now?" Ransom asked.

"I do, actually. Why is it so easy to talk to strangers and tell them your business?"

"Because talking to a stranger is not as embarrassing as talking to someone who knows you well, and there's less judgment."

"Hmm...makes sense."

The bartender dropped their drinks onto the bar, and Ransom handed over a few bills. "Keep the change."

Sophie closed salmon-pink lips around the little straw and took a sip, and his groin tightened at the thought of her wrapping those same plump lips around him and sucking.

"Good?"

"Delicious." She stirred the spritzer and took another quick sip. "Now you know all about me, how about sharing a little about you? Are you in the Bahamas for business or pleasure?"

"A little bit of both. I'm here for a wedding."

"Are you in the wedding business?"

She uncrossed and crossed her legs, drawing his eyes. Ransom wondered if she did that on purpose.

She had to know she had amazing legs—shapely, toned, and definitely eye-catching.

"The bride and groom are colleagues of mine."

"Oh really? What do you do? Wait, let me guess. Banking?"

"No."

"Are you a consultant of some kind?"

"You could say that."

Her eyebrows arrowed down. "Okay, tell me."

"I'm a civil attorney for a law firm out of Chicago. I protect my clients against frivolous lawsuits. Wait a minute, what was that look?"

Sophie fixed her face. "What look?"

"The look you just gave me, as if I'm scum and all of a sudden you wish you hadn't agreed to have a drink with me."

"Scum might be a bit of an exaggeration," she said, her gaze scurrying away from his.

"But?" Ransom prompted.

"Okay, I might as well come clean. I sort of suspected you were an attorney, but I hoped you weren't. The a-hole I told you about…he's a lawyer, too. Interestingly enough, he says civil attorneys are among the worst of the lot. You don't exactly have a good reputation." She wrinkled her round little nose.

"I'm a little offended," Ransom said, mildly amused but accustomed to people either being impressed by his profession or viewing him with suspicion. "Everyone deserves representation."

"You're not the least bit concerned about the poor individuals being taken advantage of?"

"Poor individuals?" he scoffed, plastering an exaggerated expression of shock on his face.

Sophie laughed, and her entire face lit up. She

twirled a lock of silky-looking hair around a finger. "Oh right, you're on the side of the companies. But come on, all lawsuits are *not* frivolous."

"The vast majority of them are, trust me."

"A man who truly enjoys his work, I see." She swirled the thin straw in her glass. "Don't you feel any guilt at all?" She sipped the spritzer, eyeing him through her lashes, blatantly flirtatious.

"Like I said, everyone deserves representation."

"Are you telling me you have zero guilt?"

"None whatsoever. If I didn't represent these companies, someone else would. If you saw the way people try to squeeze my clients dry for millions of dollars, often due to their own negligence, you'd understand."

She studied him for a moment, eyes soft, chin resting on her hand. "I guess we'll have to agree to disagree. Do you enjoy your work?"

That was a tough question. In the early years, he did, but nowadays he considered practicing law a means to an end. His profession allowed him to live a different life from the one he'd known, growing up on a struggling farm in Oklahoma. He drove a luxury vehicle, owned a condo in the commercial core of the third most populous city in the country, and had a closet filled with enough high-end suits to open a men's clothing store. So while the thrill of winning was no longer there, he earned a more-than-comfortable living. The career he really wanted to pursue—the one that no one knew about—could not offer him the lifestyle he now enjoyed.

"After practicing for eleven years, I make a good living," he said. "What about you? Do you enjoy your job?"

"Most days."

"What days do you not like it?"

"When we're disrespected or treated like slaves. Or when we're diminished to being mere sex objects instead of professionals with a job to do."

"Does that happen a lot?"

"Often enough that it's bothersome, but not enough to make me quit."

His eyes flicked over her, appreciating her curvaceous body. Round hips. Full breasts. He understood why men might view her in a sexual way. She was certainly easy on the eyes.

Sophie groaned. "Not you, too."

"What do you mean?"

"The way you looked at me is exactly the kind of thing I hate."

"You're wrong about me."

"It was in the eyes." She pointed two fingers at hers.

"Oh, the eyes. What else do you see in my eyes, Sophie?" He folded his arms on the bar and leaned closer—unnecessarily so—to feel her out. She didn't move away. In fact, she shifted closer.

"I see a man who probably works very hard," she said, voice dipping lower.

The corners of his mouth tipped up into a slow smile. "I do work hard, and I'm very good at what I do. Sometimes I need to let off a little steam."

"Would you like to let off some steam now?" she purred.

"As a matter of fact, I would."

She tilted her head. "What did you have in mind?"

His lurid thoughts might be too much for her right now. "I'm open to suggestions. What would you like to do tonight?"

"Are you asking me out on a date?"

"Only if you'd say yes."

She clasped her hands atop her knee. "I haven't had dinner yet."

"Well then, we should get you fed."

Her eyes narrowed. "You're not going to get me into any trouble, are you?"

"We're in the Bahamas. Of course there's going to be trouble." He enjoyed teasing her.

"Getting into trouble is not exactly my forte."

"Lucky for you, it happens to be mine. So why don't you keep a lonely attorney company?"

"I don't believe you're lonely."

"I won't be if you're with me."

Sophie pursed her lips, thinking. "All right. Where to?" she asked.

"Follow me."

He extended his arm, she took it, and they left.

Chapter Four

Sophie wasn't very hungry. She just wanted to spend more time with Ransom. He intrigued her. Turned out he wasn't very hungry either, as he'd eaten at the wedding reception. They settled on the Sea Glass lounge, located at The Cove Atlantis, which served tapas and a signature collection of cocktails.

"Mmm." Sophie raised the glass to the waiter after tasting her martini. The strawberry-infused drink contained the perfect balance of fruit flavor, gin, and vermouth.

She tucked into her arugula salad, picking up a wedge of grapefruit and a slice of beet with the fork. Across the table, Ransom ignored his small plate of braised short ribs, studying her. She quirked a brow at him.

"How long have you been a vegetarian?" he asked.

She chewed slowly and swallowed. It always amused her how curious other people were about her diet, something she considered mundane.

"Since I was sixteen. My mother is a nutritionist, which means I grew up eating healthy, with an appreciation of food and how it affects our well-being. She taught me much better than she realized. I took her admonishments to heart—maybe too much." She laughed. At his curious expression, she expounded. "By the time I was thirteen, I no longer ate red meat. Then I started doing research on the benefits of a plant-based diet. By the time I was sixteen, I had cut out all meat and seafood."

"And you haven't had any meat since you were sixteen?" He sounded surprised. He ate a morsel of the short ribs, and a bit of the brown sauce stayed on his lower lip. He lapped it up with his tongue, and Sophie caught her breath.

Damn.

She cleared her throat. "Um, not exactly. My freshman year in college, I was craving a cheeseburger and decided to satisfy the craving. Just that one time. Bad idea." She shivered at the memory. "The beef wreaked havoc with my stomach. Without going into the science of it, I shocked my digestive system and was sick for days. My mother warned me that if I wanted to try meat again, I needed to ease into it with smaller portions and something lean, like fish or chicken breasts." She popped a piece of arugula in her mouth with her fingers, enjoying the slightly bitter taste. "On rare occasions—and I do mean rare, like count-on-one-hand rare—I get a craving, but honestly, it's been so long, I don't miss meat. If I ever plan to dip my toes back in, I would do it in a much smarter way than I did fifteen years ago."

"How long have you been a flight attendant?" He

set the empty plate, cleaned of all the meat, off to the side. Despite not being hungry, he clearly had a healthy appetite.

"Nine years and counting."

"Is that what you've always wanted to do?"

"Before I started working for Noble Airlines, no. But now, I love what I do. I've met everyone from celebrities to teachers to...you name it. I like meeting different people, and I get to travel at a very, very low cost. Before, I used to manage my mother's shop. She runs a juice and smoothie bar in Atlanta. Now, in any given week, I'm chilling poolside in Miami or hiking the Smoky Mountains of Tennessee. I visit Paris regularly, where I have to make a stop at my favorite bakery in the sixth arrondissement for their flaky, buttery croissants and to-die-for desserts, and just two months ago I was sipping a cold drink on a beach in the Virgin Islands. Life couldn't be better."

"It's not all great trips and flexible schedules," Ransom said. "You must have some crazy stories to tell, like that jerk who almost took your arm."

"I do have some crazy stories. I could tell you about the passenger who sat in the middle of the aisle and wouldn't move because he couldn't get the seat he wanted. We had to have him escorted off the plane. And I can't tell you how many times couples have tried to join the mile-high club. That happens more often than I'd like."

"You're kidding."

"Nope. You wouldn't believe the things I've seen," Sophie said dryly, with a roll of her eyes.

Ransom maintained direct eye contact, his big body relaxed in the chair, one hand resting at the base of the martini glass on the table, the other on the chair's armrest.

Sophie played with the idea of a quick fling before she went back to the States, to soothe her bruised ego. Ransom would be the perfect person to console her.

"I feel like I've been talking about myself all night," she said.

"Nothing wrong with that. I like listening to your voice. It's very sexy."

His comment made her blush. She missed this type of interaction with a man. The flirting and teasing had long disappeared from her own relationship.

"I happen to like your voice, too." Sophie rested her forearms on the table and leaned toward him, an instinctive response to seek closer contact. "Tell me an interesting story about your job. I know you have some."

"I'm just a boring attorney," he said, a twinkle in his eyes.

"I do not believe that. Come on. Tell me something fun or interesting. Do you ever get to travel?" She really did want to know more.

"On occasion. I'm one of the top litigators in my firm, and my work sometimes takes me to other countries. Last year a Japanese company got into a legal dispute with some of the workers at their subsidiary in Chicago. My team and I spent three weeks in Tokyo, advising the Japanese attorneys on how to handle the case. Let's see..." He dragged a thumb across his lower lip, and Sophie's eyes followed the surprisingly sexy movement. "A couple of years ago I flew back and forth to Paris for six months, helping a French consumer products firm navigate our legal system after a children's advocacy group sued them for making false claims in their ads. Unfortunately, I didn't get to see much of Tokyo or Paris."

"Why not?"

"Too busy working."

Sophie pouted. "That's a shame," she murmured.

"You worried about me, Sophie?"

She tuned out the other diners and concentrated on the way he said her name. The way he spoke. Firm, succinct words in a low tenor that made the inside of her belly flutter.

"A little. You sound like one of those workaholics who misses out on life." Like her boyfriend, Keith.

"I'm postponing the fun until a later date. How's that?" He took a drink from the martini glass. The muscles beneath his shirt moved with the controlled movement.

"Not much better, but I'll give you a pass."

He chuckled, a low, masculine sound.

"So…with all this work you do, I guess you don't have a girlfriend? Or a wife?"

"I recently ended a relationship and have no plans to enter another one. Too distracting. Too many demands on my time."

Sophie's stomach clenched and she broke eye contact. She barely knew Ransom, yet his answer disappointed her. Rather than examine the unexpected feeling, she rested her chin in her hand. "What's next?" she asked.

"Breakfast." He smiled at her from across the table. Not a full-on smile, but a sort of sexy, wicked hint of a smile that displayed deep lines in his cheeks.

"Excuse me?"

"It's the least I could do after I take you to bed."

The audacious remark left her breathless and a little aroused. Her nipples tightened. "How can you be sure that'll happen?"

He shrugged. "It's what we both want." He exuded confidence and a certain amount of arrogance. He knew he was the shit.

Sophie laughed. "You, sir, are being rather presumptuous."

"Am I?" His gaze locked with hers.

She took a steady breath, the apex of her thighs throbbing, answering the hunger she saw reflected in his eyes.

"I'm a little disappointed." She pursed her lips. She would not make it that easy for him, and intended to prolong the wait and extend the verbal foreplay they'd been engaged in for the past few hours. Even as the thought crossed her mind, she was shocked to realize that she'd made up her mind to sleep with him.

"Why are you disappointed?" he asked.

"I thought a lawyer...someone who claims to be successful at what he does, would present a better argument."

"I can be very persuasive. And patient," he added, as if he knew exactly what she was up to. "What would you like to do next?"

She pretended to think about the options, though she already had an idea. "Dancing would be fun." She'd heard the nightclub upstairs from the casino served up great drinks and great music. It was a popular spot for hotel guests and islanders.

His eyes ran over her breasts and arms, and the heated gaze warmed her skin everywhere it landed. "I'd love to watch you dance," he said huskily.

Everything he said sounded like a seduction, and

she fell deeper and deeper under his spell.

"Then let's go, and I'll show you my moves."

****

She didn't say no to breakfast.

That was Ransom's thought as he followed Sophie up the stairs to the nine-thousand-square-foot nightclub and watched her hips sway in front of him.

Purple and red lights flashed over the crowd as they entered. Near the door, an ebony-skinned woman danced on a raised platform in a sparkling blue bikini. She worked her toned body back and forth, whipping a waist-length ponytail around her head in a circle.

"Come on, let's dance," Sophie said, taking Ransom's hand.

The music in the club pumped hard enough that he had difficulty hearing, but he read her lips easily enough.

Ransom shook his head. He pulled her close, so that not only his breath but his lips touched her ear when he spoke. She smelled flowery, her skin sprayed with a fragrance that made him want to press his nose into her neck. This was the closest he'd been to her all night, and he slipped a possessive arm around her waist, marking her as his for anyone paying attention.

"*We* are not going dancing. I don't dance." He had two left feet and no rhythm.

She lifted her eyes to his. "Then why did you agree to come here?"

He pulled her closer again, very aware of her. The jasmine notes in her perfume. The soft curve in her back where his hand rubbed up and down her spine.

His body tightened in response. "To spend time with you," he said, making direct eye contact.

She shivered against him, and he let his hand fall away. She remained transfixed, speechless and looking up at him. He nudged her forward with his hand. "Go on. Have fun."

She licked her lips, teasing him the way he'd done her, before dancing off into the crowd.

Tables and cushioned benches lined the walls, and Ransom found an empty place to sit with a good view of the floor and the bar on the other side of the room. All around him men and women moved to the music and laughed, having a good time.

He stopped a server when she walked by and ordered a mixed drink. Then his gaze drifted around the room and landed on Sophie, kicking up her heels. She smiled up at her dance partner, teasing him with her sultry eyes and a secretive smile on her lush mouth. The more he watched, the more he noticed.

Clearly the kind of woman who tended to be the life of the party, she downright glowed in the dimness of the club. Her undulating figure stood out in the bright sundress against the golden yellow of her skin. The dress clung to her hips and the swell of her derriere as she twisted and gyrated, hands in the air, shimmying low and then twisting back up again.

High-heeled gold sandals elongated her legs and showed off her calves. His gaze stayed on those legs for a long time, imagining them locked around his waist. Her head tossed back. His mouth on her neck and his hands gripping her hips as he drove into her trembling body. He imagined her gasping and pleading and begging him to drive harder, an image so vivid that for several long seconds he stopped breathing. Lost in the fantasy of fucking her breathless.

Ransom shifted positions on the seat and flagged down the server to order another drink. By the time Sophie joined him, he had his body under better control.

"Whew, that was fun." She plopped down next to him.

"Don't tell me you're finished?" he asked, extending an arm along the back of the seat. His fingers played along the line of her shoulder. She had soft skin.

"Oh no, I'm going back out there." She glowed under the colorful lights. Her cheeks were flushed a becoming pink color, and her eyes sparkled. She fanned her face. "I needed to take a quick break."

"Let me buy you a drink."

"Water for now."

"You're a cheap date," Ransom teased.

He flagged down the server and Sophie ordered a water and, at Ransom's insistence, a Nassau tea, similar to a Long Island tea but made with Blue Curaçao.

During the next three or so hours, a steady stream of top-forty hits dominated the DJ's selections, and even though Ransom occasionally checked his phone, more often than not, his eyes were drawn to Sophie out in the middle of the club. She lost herself in the music and put her all into dancing. That vivaciousness made it so that she was never without a partner, and he could only imagine how that energy would translate into the bedroom.

Late in the night, the music shifted to selections with slower beats, and Sophie came to sit beside him.

"Are you hungry?" Ransom asked.

She picked up the menu and perused it. "I don't see anything I want except the potato skins, and they have bacon on them. I'll be fine with just some water."

Ransom flagged down the waitress. "Two waters and a platter of chicken tenders for me." He pointed at the menu. "Can we get the potato skins without bacon?"

"Um…I'm not sure," the waitress said.

"I'll make it worth your while if you can make that happen." He flashed a grin.

The young lady blushed. "I'll see what I can do."

"Appreciate it."

Leaning close, Sophie said, "You didn't have to do that."

Ransom shrugged. He didn't, but he'd wanted to. "It's no big deal."

She bit her bottom lip and her eyes softened. "That was very sweet. Thank you."

Ransom swallowed past the tightness in his throat. He rubbed her arm. "My pleasure."

Minutes later, the waitress set the food and water on the table in front of them.

"Pretty soon they'll be kicking us out," Sophie said, taking a bite of a baconless potato skin.

She should be tired after being up for almost twenty-four hours and spending so much time dancing, but she felt very much alive. Her heart raced and skin tingled with excitement. No doubt her mood was influenced by the man beside her.

Ransom reached across the back of the seat and pushed his hand under her hair, letting his fingers massage the nape of her neck. She leaned into the pressure of his hand, and aching need compounded between her thighs.

During the many hours they'd spent together, he had touched her often. Her shoulder. Her arm. Her wrist. Each touch eroded her resistance to him. Not that she'd really been trying to resist him, but their time together was a delicate dance of showing interest without appearing too eager. And his constant touching made her eager—very eager—and over the course of minutes, a definite shift had taken place.

They'd been circling each other all night, simply waiting for the right moment when they were completely in sync.

That moment was now.

Ransom pulled her in and pressed his mouth into hers. A gentle probing, almost as if testing her. Of their own accord, her fingers flattened against his hard chest, exploring the muscles and the firmness of his broad shoulders. Breathlessly, she opened her mouth and allowed his tongue to sink between her lips. Hers darted toward him, sliding and twisting in a bold greeting. Then his mouth firmed and he applied more pressure, and she pushed into the kiss, moaning softly.

He hadn't removed his hand from the back of her neck. He kept it there in a casual manner, and his warm palm clasped her skin and pooled heat in her loins.

His other hand slid beneath her dress and pulled her legs apart. Her heart jolted. She tried to close her legs, but he pulled them apart again, placing a firm hand on her sensitive inner thigh and letting his hand climb even higher. Sophie gasped into his mouth as excitement pulsed like a drum in her core.

His lips left hers to nip the corner of her mouth, pluck her full bottom lip between his teeth, and move across her jaw down the side of her neck. Sophie's eyes fluttered half-closed and she arched her back, uncaring of their location and uncaring that the table in front of them barely covered their actions. She was solely focused on the movement of his hand and moist mouth.

Ransom brought his lips to her ear. "Since the flight I've imagined you naked, and all night I've wanted to take you out of this dress and spread your legs." He squeezed her bare thigh, and he flicked his tongue against the corner of her mouth, seducing her with words and touch. "Would you like to spread your legs for me?"

A flicker of doubt threatened to derail the seduction. Struggling to breathe, Sophie let her gaze meet his. "I have a boyfriend."

He didn't flinch. "That's his problem, not mine."

He kissed her again while his hand moved higher to trace the edge of her panties at the crease of her hips. A charge of hot lust speared her sex, and Sophie whimpered, trembling at the light caress.

"I would only be using you." Her voice came out ragged and hoarse.

"Maybe I'm using you."

Her entire body tingled with anticipation. She'd been moving toward this very moment from the minute she approached Ransom at the roulette table.

Revenge sex. The perfect way to pay back Keith for what he'd done, and reward herself in the process.

"In that case, let's use each other."

Chapter Five

They burst into Ransom's room, mouths and hands clinging to each other as they fumbled to remove their constricting clothes. Sophie had a vague sense of the grandeur of his suite as they stumbled over the floor of the parlor into the adjoining bedroom. Punches of orange and yellow whizzed by the corners of her eyes in the dimly lit room, but she couldn't be bothered to pay close attention, too busy moaning with pleasure as Ransom sucked the base of her neck, brushing his nose along the curve of her throat while squeezing her aching breasts in his big hands.

He edged her toward the bed with his hips, the delicious, insistent pressure of his erection prodding her stomach. He looped an arm around her back and tugged down the zipper of her dress, licking her collarbone as he did in one wickedly erotic sweep that made her get up on her toes for more. The dress fell around her ankles when he tugged it down her arms, and she stood before him in heels, a taupe bra with lace trim, and the matching thong, basking in the heat of his appreciative gaze.

Nostrils flaring, he took a moment to sweep his eyes over her breasts to her hips. He looked like he wanted to devour her, and she wanted to be devoured.

"Incredible," he muttered.

With a flick of a finger, Ransom released the front clasp of her bra and her breasts tumbled from confinement, the aching, pointed tips tightening in the air. He cupped the soft mounds and squeezed them together, pressing his mouth against the top curve and rubbing his thumbs along the taut nipples. His soft hair brushed her chin and collarbone, and the beginning of stubble grated her sensitive skin.

Sophie held her breath, barely able to endure the swell of need he unleashed, trembling on the cusp of a new and wild experience. Relentless fire beat through her veins, forcing her to tear at his shirt, exposing his hard chest even as he fastened his lips over hers again.

She forced him into a deeper kiss, leaning into his mouth. His heavenly, moist mouth. Soft with the right amount of force. He kissed her thoroughly and with enthusiasm, nipping at the corners and sucking her bottom lip. He took his time, concentrating as if to get it just right. And it was perfect. The gentle tugging, coupled with his hand drifting down to her lower back, built heated pressure in her pelvis. Her nipples contracted into aching peaks as she drowned in the minty-fresh scent of him.

"Sophie, Sophie." He hooked his thumbs in the

waistband of her thong. "The things I want to do to you…"

Her breath stuttered as he dragged the lingerie past her knees and she stepped out. Then he stood back and looked at her, shaking his head. "Breathtaking," he muttered.

She delighted in the way he stared at her nakedness. His eyes darkened into deep blue and ran over her as if he'd never been as captivated by another woman's body.

Reaching for his pants, she whispered, "You're overdressed."

They stripped his clothes off until he was as naked as she, and his body was a sight to behold. Simply gorgeous. Even more magnificent than she'd expected, boasting a lean waist, firm biceps, and rock-hard abs. His full-on erection was couched between two thighs the size of tree trunks, muscled and chiseled like the planes of his chest and abdomen.

Colorful tattoos covered his shoulder to the middle of his forearm and over to his left pec. She ran a hand over the designs, but there wasn't time to explore or examine. She kicked off her shoes and fell onto the bed. Ransom followed her down, the welcome weight of him pushing her into the mattress.

His pink tongue rubbed over the tops of her sensitive breasts before claiming the nipple of the left one. His mouth closed over it like a warm clasp, and Sophie moaned low and deep in her throat, arching her back. That seemed to be the constant position of her body—arching and reaching and straining toward him.

Her fingers tunneled into his hair, holding him tight as he sucked and pulled with his lips and teeth.

He ravaged the tender flesh and then laved the puckered skin with his tongue, the soothing motion equally erotic. He drove her body crazy. So crazy she could barely stand the heated sensations barreling under her skin.

The sensual onslaught continued, focused on her breasts while his hand dragged in the valley between them, over her stomach and between her legs to the mound of curly hair below.

"Spread those legs for me," he said.

And she obeyed, her legs falling wide. He fingered her opening and her body jolted. He electrified her skin and sent shock waves to her extremities.

His hand moved between her legs and swirled in the wetness around her moist clit. He circled the nub, going wide at first and playing with the lips. Then he massaged even faster, making the circles even tighter. She wiggled against his hand, whimpering and begging. He stroked and caressed, taunting her until she gasped and her head rolled back into the pillows.

She bit her lower lip and sank her fingers into the muscles of his back. The apex of her thighs became a throbbing mass of hunger.

"I can't wait to get inside you."

He whispered the hot words into her skin and removed his hand from between her legs. She lifted her hips high, silently begging him to put it back.

Ransom traveled down her torso, his hands and mouth turning her inside out with soft caresses and moist licks along her waist and hips. A quick kiss to her clit sent a surge of heat to her sex and made her growl in exasperation as he went lower still, down to her knees, and even ventured as low as the arch of her foot. He bathed her in kisses. Pleasurable, out-of-this-world kisses that made her stretch and preen as she savored each one. She was breathless and boneless and filled with desire for him.

Finally, he offered what she so desperately wanted. Donning a condom, he entered her in a rush, eager to possess her. Long and wide, he hit every spot as he sank deep. The pleasure of his invasion made her throw back her head in abandon.

His hands gripped her thighs and she lifted her knees to his waist. Sophie crossed her arms at the back of his strong neck, thrusting upward, demanding he give her more.

Her body went haywire as he drove hard and deep. Alternating speed, he thrust very, very fast and then frustratingly slow, withdrawing to the tip and then plunging to the hilt. But no matter the speed, he felt so good. Unbelievably good.

"Damn, you feel incredible," he whispered as he fucked her.

He shifted her ankle onto his shoulder and she bore the slight discomfort to take him even deeper at that new angle. He squeezed her breast and pulled it into his mouth to suck on the hard bud of a nipple. Sophie gripped his rock-hard body tight, her hands smoothing over the rippling muscles beneath his skin.

His mouth was on her breast, her leg around his neck, and his body driving, driving into hers with each insistent rock of his hips.

The ache between her thighs grew tighter and tighter until the pressure built and she splintered, shattering as he hit it just right. Her muscles pulsed around him as wave after wave of pleasure lashed along her nerves.

"That's it, sweetheart. Come on this cock." His

tongue rubbed her stinging nipple.

The words…his tongue…the constant drive of his body into hers…

Another orgasm blasted through her, and Sophie gasped and cried out. Multiples. That rare, elusive unicorn.

Her second climax seemed to undo him. His hips lost their rhythm and he unleashed a litany of curse words against her chest.

In the aftermath, all she could think was that it was insane, this type of bliss. Mind-numbing. Sending her emotions careening out of control and her body trembling until it literally ached from the intense pleasure.

****

Watching Ransom come back into the room, Sophie pulled the sheet over her exposed breasts. The soft cotton felt like sandpaper against her humming body.

He climbed into the bed, a glint brightening his eyes. "Were you satisfied?" he asked.

As if he didn't know. "Are you asking because you want a pat on the back or because you're concerned about my satisfaction?"

Ransom smirked, the twin dimples sinking deep into his cheeks. "Both."

He eased the sheet lower on her waist, and her nipples pebbled under the exposure.

"You're so responsive," he said, flattening his hand over her ribs, right below her breasts.

Sophie swallowed, moving a little restlessly in response to his touch. She'd never been like this with other men. Ransom seemed to have some kind of erotic hold over her.

He gently kissed her arm. "It'll be daylight soon, and we should get some rest, but…" He covered one breast with his hand and her restless movements intensified. She gasped when she felt his hardening penis bump her outer thigh. "I want you again."

"Again?" she whispered. She wanted him, too. Sleep was the last thing on her mind.

"Mhmm."

While he nibbled on her neck and ear, he eased her onto her stomach.

Oh god. Her favorite position. She was already wet and getting wetter by the second.

Ransom reached for a condom and tested her readiness with a sweep of his hand between her thighs. "On your hands and knees," he instructed in a thick voice.

Quivering with anticipation, Sophie sank her hands and knees into the mattress and lifted her ass toward him.

He swept her hair away from her nape and sank his teeth into her neck. She curled her body back, lifting her bottom into the hardness of his length. One hand on her hip yanked her even tighter against him, and he mashed her breasts together with one hand while thrusting hard against her ass.

"What are you doing to me?" she whispered.

She reached back for him, her body quaking beneath the strength of his.

"Giving you what you deserve." Ransom shoved into her.

Sophie could no longer stand the combination of sensations. The rough handling and layers of sexual stimulation were almost too much. She sank onto her forearms.

"A good fucking," he said. He widened his legs between hers and sprawled her beneath him.

With one hand on her neck, he drove into her. She exploded almost instantly, cheek to the pillow, eyes shut tight and crying out with a loud voice. He used her body but offered so much in return. Yes, he demanded her submission, but he delivered unparalleled satisfaction, in a splendor of sensation that left her shaking and sobbing with pleasure.

Chapter Six

Sophie's eyes fluttered open. A lock of hair obscured her vision, and she squinted against the morning light, experiencing a level of contentment she hadn't felt in a long time. She noted the pillows strewn across the bed, the sheets bunched up around her legs, and the hair-sprinkled male arm thrown across her waist.

She shoved a curly tendril of hair out of her face to clear her vision and stretched, loosening her limbs and working out the minor aches in her muscles as she groaned.

Ransom's arms tightened and tucked her back closer into his chest. Any closer and she'd be absorbed into his skin.

The position felt normal and natural, like a couple who'd spent many years together. The intimacy of lying around naked, wrapped in each other's arms, skin to skin, was another aspect of her current relationship she missed. Keith was always running off because he had an early meeting or needed to catch up on work. Most times she felt dismissed after sex, lying in bed alone, when the desire to touch and be touched was strongest.

She ran her fingers through the hairs on Ransom's forearm, playfully tugging until he grunted his displeasure.

"I have to get up. I'm going on a tour today," she said.

"I thought about going on a tour myself."

His low voice sounded lower after several hours of sleep, and she pressed back even farther against him, burying herself into the warmth of the sound. There was so much contradictory stimuli in this early morning cuddle. The soft mattress, but his hard body. The cool sheets, but his warm skin pressed into her back and thighs. Contented heat radiated in Sophie's chest.

"When do you leave the island?" she asked.

"Tomorrow morning, bright and early." He yawned.

Sophie's fingers stilled, and a knot of despondency settled between her shoulders. She wanted to prolong her time with him.

"We could go on a tour together," she suggested lightly, her stomach knotted. She didn't know how he would respond to such a suggestion. Perhaps their night together was a one-time thing.

"Good idea," he said, and rolled onto his back. "What did you have in mind?"

Plopping onto her back, Sophie assessed his appearance. Strands of hair tumbled across his brow, in utter disarray on his head. She combed her fingers through his messy hair, taking pleasure in the softness and texture.

"A tour of Nassau, for sure. After that, we can play it by ear."

He yawned again and scrubbed a hand over his hair-roughened face. "Then I guess we better get up."

Whimpering like a petulant child, she turned onto her side and yanked a pillow over her head.

"Come on, birthday girl."

Her eyes flew open and her heart leapt. He remembered.

Ransom smacked her butt and she yelped from the tender pain. "You said you wanted to see the island—let's go see the island."

They rolled out of bed and agreed to meet in forty minutes for breakfast. Sophie left, but first he planted a firm, sensual kiss on her lips.

In her own room, she showered and changed into an apricot halter and a pair of white capris with tennis shoes. After dressing, she picked up the phone she'd left on the dresser and saw numerous texts and calls from her boyfriend, Keith. He'd been trying to reach her all night, sent an early morning text, and left a voicemail while she slept in the bed with Ransom.

I want to see you.

Don't you think you've punished me enough?

Why aren't you returning my calls?

On and on they went. The voicemails were more of the same. She was tempted to call or at least send him a text, but didn't bother when she realized that not one of those communications wished her a happy birthday. He hadn't remembered, and his negligence was a tart reminder of the many reasons why their relationship had so many problems.

Sophie turned off the phone and placed it in the room safe. She would not take it with her. No distractions while touring today. If her parents needed to reach her, they knew her room number, but she doubted they'd call. They'd encouraged her to take the trip and enjoy herself for her birthday, and that was exactly what she planned to do.

She and Ransom left the hotel, the first order of business being a tour of Nassau, which took them on a colorful journey that filled them in on the history of the islands and their pirate influences. They sampled a variety of spirits and enjoyed handmade chocolates from Graycliff Chocolatier, an interactive chocolate factory where they learned how cacao beans were processed. As part of the tour, they even created their own uniquely flavored chocolate pieces. At John Watling's Distillery on Delancy Street, named after a pirate, they toured the facility and learned about handcrafted rum and other spirits made by the Bahamians. Sophie purchased souvenirs and bottles of pale rum and amber rum, made on the premises from local ingredients.

They stopped to eat at a restaurant off the beaten path, but highly recommended by the guide. Tucked away behind historic buildings, the outdoor patio of Cafe Matisse provided the perfect ambiance for a late lunch. While Ransom dug into the mixed seafood platter with herb sauce, Sophie received the special treatment when the chef prepared a dish not on the menu—sautéed vegetables in a creamy cheese sauce—and personally brought it to the table to gauge her enjoyment.

She thanked him profusely. Lucky for her, chefs often wanted the opportunity to experiment, and creating unique dishes for people with dietary restrictions was an opportunity for them to shine. She'd indulged in some tasty one-of-a-kind dishes over the years, and this one was no exception.

Watching Ransom, she couldn't help but notice that he ate in much the same way he approached sex—with gusto and enthusiasm. He devoured the garlic bread the same way he'd devoured her. He licked a drop of sauce from his thumb with the same tongue that had licked the tips of her breasts. She wanted to climb onto his lap watching the way he dived into the meal.

She and Ransom chatted as they lingered over crème brûlée and coffee, and argued about politics.

"What do you do for fun?" he asked at one point, sipping his coffee.

"I travel." She smirked.

"When you're not traveling, smartass."

His blue eyes smiled into hers, and a painful ache pierced her chest at the thought that tomorrow he'd be gone from her life for good. Sophie shifted her gaze to the glass of water on the table and corralled her emotions before answering.

"When I'm in Atlanta, I ride my bicycle. There's a bike shop near my mother's juice shop in Midtown, and I'm a member of a cycle club that meets there and rides out every Saturday morning."

"That explains your sexy-ass legs."

"You're just full of compliments," she said, grinning across the table at him. "I don't ride as often as I'd like. Sometimes I help my mother at the shop, but most weekends I go out with the club when I'm not traveling."

"I haven't gotten as far as riding with a club yet."

"You ride?"

"Like you, not as often as I'd like. Work keeps me busy."

"You should make time, if you enjoy it. A club is a good way to get involved, and I'm sure they have active ones in Chicago."

He nodded. "Maybe I will."

Satisfied and bellies full, they headed back to the hotel and spent the afternoon in or near the water: parasailing—a first for Sophie—and then a competitive game of beach volleyball with another couple. Ransom dominated the game, diving for the ball and spiking on their opponents. After a sound thrashing, the other couple turned down the offer of a rematch and ran off down the beach.

"You kicked their asses," Sophie said, lifting her hands above her head and doing a little victory wiggle.

"We did," Ransom said.

"You didn't even need me. You won all by yourself."

"It's you. You're still bringing me good luck." Ransom growled and grabbed her around the thighs, lifting her into a quick spin on the sand.

Throwing her arms around his neck, Sophie squealed as he raced toward the ocean. They splashed around, swimming and chasing each other in the water. A group of kids joined them, and they played a game of water tag until the children's parents called them to head back to the room. Ransom and Sophie then returned to their cabana on the beach.

The smell of the salt water and the screams of laughing children lulled Sophie into an afternoon nap. She didn't know how long she'd been asleep, but Ransom's hand on her shoulder woke her up. He sat with his legs swung over the side of the lounge chair.

"I need to go back to my room and check emails and get a little bit of work done," he said.

Sophie pouted, looking up at him from a reclining position behind her sunglasses. "You can't be serious," she said.

"Us horrible attorneys have to work hard all the time," he said.

She wrinkled her nose at him. "I hope you weren't offended by my comments when we met."

"No, but you can still make it up to me later," he said with a wicked smile, the twin slashes in his cheeks making an appearance. He dropped a kiss to her lips.

Sophie flipped the shades onto her forehead. "Life is short, you know. You shouldn't spend it working all the time."

His eyes narrowed on her. "This is going to sound crazy, but I haven't been this relaxed in a long time. My vacations aren't usually real vacations."

"Then you should take real vacations more often."

"Maybe one day." He squeezed her toes, and the non-erotic pressure still managed to feel very erotic. "But I have a plan, and I need to stay focused on it."

"And what's that?"

"Making partner. I'm this close." He held a finger and thumb a penny's width apart.

"No straying from the plan?" she asked, keeping her voice mild and face neutral. She didn't want to judge, but she thought his focus bordered on obsessive.

"No straying from the plan," Ransom confirmed.

Sophie swung her feet over the side of the chair so their knees were almost touching. "Come on, you'll be back at work tomorrow. Spend the rest of the afternoon with me. There are two Jet Skis with our names on them."

Ransom's brow knitted into a thoughtful frown. "I've never been on a Jet Ski before."

"Well, sir, you simply must have that experience, and what better time than the present." She leaned closer, making sure to take full advantage of the cleavage above her bikini top. She dropped her voice. "Trust me. It's an out-of-this-world experience you don't want to miss because you're stuck in your room *working*, of all things."

Behind his sunglasses, she saw his eyes dip to her chest. "Oh yeah?"

"I promise."

"I wouldn't want you on opposing counsel. You make a very compelling argument." The blunt tip of his middle finger swiped lightly over her breasts.

Her nipples tingled and her toes curled into the sand. "Does that mean I can look forward to spending more time with you this afternoon?" she said, running a hand over one of his thighs. She enjoyed the role of femme fatale, teasing and cajoling him to do her will. Knowing they'd never see each other again emboldened her.

"And the evening," Ransom added. "How about dinner, and more...stimulating conversation in my suite later?"

"I like your plan," Sophie said.

They spent the rest of the afternoon together in the sun and in the water, ending the day on Jet Skis, and afterward finally separated, agreeing to meet up at seven for dinner.

In her room, Sophie pondered the day. For most

of it, she hadn't thought about her boyfriend, and while she did experience some guilt for having sex with Ransom, she didn't regret what she'd done. Would Keith have regretted sleeping with the waitress if she hadn't discovered the lewd texts on his phone?

Ransom was an amazing lover, exciting and sexy, and paid her the attention she'd been craving for a long time. Tomorrow he'd be leaving, and as time ticked by, she contemplated broaching the topic of staying in touch. He could be a backup plan, in case Keith didn't act right again.

Her cheeks heated. The thought of hooking up with Ransom again was ludicrous. Theirs was a one-time experience and not meant to be repeated. Besides, she lived in Atlanta. Ransom lived in Chicago. While he seemed to enjoy her company, that didn't mean he'd want to stay in touch.

She pulled on a spaghetti-strap white dress and silver sandals, and was in the middle of pulling her hair into a topknot when a knock sounded at the door. A quick glance at the clock told her that it was quarter to seven. Ransom was early. She smiled at her reflection, anxious to see him, the ever-present flutter in her belly evidence of how much she looked forward to his company.

Broadening her smile into a welcoming grin, Sophie flung open the door, but her smile collapsed like a house of cards, and she froze, gaping at the man standing on the other side. Shock ricocheted through her insides as she stared at the familiar face.

Instead of blue eyes, she saw dark chocolate. Instead of lustrous dark brown hair, she saw onyx black.

"What are you doing here?"

Keith Wong stood with both hands braced on the doorframe, his lanky body dressed in a chest-hugging T-shirt and jeans.

"You won't return my calls, but I came to prove to you that I'm a changed man." His smile was soft and regretful. "Happy birthday, baby."

Chapter Seven

Her voice sounded weird. The lighthearted vibrancy from earlier was gone and replaced with a guarded tone. Something was wrong.

"I'll be there in a minute and we can go to dinner," Ransom said. He had a surprise planned. He'd called the restaurant and informed them it was her birthday. They arranged to have a cake and candles ready, and the staff on hand to serenade her at the end of the meal.

"No." The single word came out fast—almost frantic.

"What's the matter, you want to cancel our dinner?" he asked half-jokingly. He looked forward to spending their last night together. In fact, he hoped it wouldn't be the last time they saw each other. True, they lived in different cities, but he'd done the long-distance thing before, and it worked well enough. He wanted a shot with Sophie, assuming she was interested and willing to dump her douchebag boyfriend.

"Something's come up."

Her voice fell even lower, and a chunk of worry landed in his gut.

"You don't sound like yourself."

"Can you just meet me somewhere else? Please. I'll explain everything when I see you."

Ransom stared at the expanse of beach and water outside the glass door. "When do you want to meet?"

"Right away."

They agreed to meet at the lobby lounge.

"I'll see you in five minutes," he said.

Hanging up the phone, he mulled the conversation, trying to figure out what could have changed. He had absolutely no idea, and the uncertainty troubled him, tightening the bundle of unease in his gut.

He picked up the box wrapped in white with a hot-pink ribbon. Inside was a conch shell necklace with a clamshell pendant covered in gold. A dusting of light pink infused each round bead. The colorful beads reminded him of Sophie and fit her style. He'd been excited when he bought the jewelry, but now he hesitated.

Shaking off the indecision, he exited the room with the box and went to the lounge. He found her sitting alone at a booth, her wavy hair up in a loose knot on her head, looking as fresh-faced as she had when she woke up in his arms this morning. But there was a shift in her demeanor. The contentment was gone and a little wrinkle in her forehead hinted at her troubling thoughts. The knot of worry settled deeper behind his abs.

Slipping into the booth, Ransom placed the gift on the table between them. Instead of showing gratitude or excitement, she parted her lips in obvious dismay—a clear indication the conversation was on a downward spiral before it even started.

"That's not exactly the reaction I expected," he said.

She briefly closed her eyes and slowly opened them. She appeared smaller, as if curling into herself, and her eyes were a dull, muted gray. No excitement in them at all.

Ransom steeled himself for the coming talk, one he clearly wouldn't enjoy.

"I had a great time with you," she said, staring at some point behind his head. She couldn't even look him in the face.

"But...?"

"You're leaving tomorrow, and it's best that we...say our goodbyes here and now."

"So it's over?" Ransom laughed, not really finding humor in the situation. He just needed a way to get rid of the nervous energy that threatened to overtake him. "We're just done?"

"Ransom—"

"We had dinner plans. At least tell me why."

Shifting in the chair, Sophie stared down at the table and chewed on her bottom lip. A lip he'd spent an unreasonable amount of time kissing and sucking because he enjoyed its softness so much.

"He's here."

She spoke in such a low voice he leaned in to hear.

"Your boyfriend?"

She nodded.

"He surprised you?"

"Yes." Her eyes flicked up to him.

Ransom fell back against the seat, shocked but also angry. He fisted a hand on the table but really wanted to slam his fist through it. "He shows up and you drop everything."

"That's not exactly what's happening."

"Then what exactly *is* happening?" he demanded, voice coarser and louder than expected.

She swallowed. "I don't know what to say. This is very awkward for me. I had no idea he would come."

"You wanted him to."

"I did not. I ignored all the messages he left. I wanted time alone."

"Then explain why you're ready to run back into his arms after you told me what an asshole this guy is."

"He came all the way down here to see me, and I can't ignore that." Her voice pleaded with him to understand.

"And us?" Ransom asked, hating the strangled sound of his voice. Hating to even ask the question like a needy punk.

"We barely know each other." Her eyes searched his.

Ransom acknowledged the truth of her words. He couldn't even begin to try to convince her to leave someone she had known for years when they had only known each other for the whopping grand total of twenty-four hours. And yes, the sex was great, but great sex did not mean they were compatible in other areas.

"You're right." He affected a smirk, to lighten the heavy mood and make her think he didn't give a shit, that he hadn't been contemplating keeping in touch and trying to see if they could work—even with the distance between them. "You're a beautiful woman, Sophie. I had a great time with you. Your boyfriend is a lucky man, and I don't blame him for coming here to surprise you. He probably figured you might run into a guy like me and he might lose you for good."

"I'm not exactly sure I've forgiven him."

"You will."

"So that's it, then?" Her voice shook a little.

"That's it. Good luck to you." He couldn't take sitting there in front of her anymore, knowing he could no longer touch her. Knowing that tonight she'd be in another man's arms so soon after he'd been thrusting inside her, so deep he never wanted to come out again.

He slid from the booth.

"Ransom, wait!" Sophie jumped up and stood before him, breathing hard, worry in her eyes. "I'm sorry. Maybe I—"

"Sorry for what?" He wasn't going to make it easy for her, because it wasn't easy for him. Unbearable tightness filled his torso, made his chest hurt and his stomach contract with intense pain. "You made the right decision going back to your boyfriend. We were both having a good time. Using each other. There was never going to be anything between us."

Her breath hitched on a sharp inhale, and a wounded expression filled her eyes. He'd done exactly as planned—hurt her by diminishing their time together to nothing more than a night of screwing that was going nowhere. And he felt like shit.

Steely resolve shifted into her features. Her jaw firmed and her spine straightened. "You're right. Clearly, I made the right decision," she said.

The verbal dig cut across him like the sharp edge of a sword.

Lips pressed together, Sophie leveled one last hard look at him and stalked away.

Ransom watched her swaying hips and beautiful legs move across the floor. When he could no longer see her, he snatched the gift from the table and rushed back to his room, almost knocking over a teenaged boy ambling along with her parents.

He slammed the door to the suite and tossed the gift onto the dresser. Standing in the middle of the room, he stared at the bed and recalled the passionate night he and Sophie spent together. The thought of her lying under another man—even one who had more right to claim her than he did—drove him insane.

He grabbed his phone but stopped before dialing her number. What could he say? There was nothing he could say. She was with the person she wanted to be with, and her decision made him furious. Furious at her. Furious at himself. Because deep down he'd wanted to not just give her great sex, but hit it so good she'd forget all about the ass who allowed her to come to the Bahamas alone.

In a rage, Ransom slammed his phone on top of the dresser, over and over again until the screen cracked and the device fell apart in his hand. Pieces flew off the furniture in multiple directions and onto the carpet.

Breathing heavily, he stared at the shattered phone. "Forget her," he muttered.

That was what he planned to do. Forget he ever laid eyes—or mouth, or hand—on Sophie Bradshaw.

****

The weight of rejection pressed down like a hand onto Sophie's sternum as she plodded back to her room. She could hardly breathe against the pressure, and stopped near her building to catch her breath and clear her head.

There was never going to be anything between us.

The brutal words crushed her, and she clutched a handful of the white dress, pressing her fist against her stomach to ease the pain.

His rejection shouldn't hurt so much. She shouldn't care so much.

She wanted to run back and tell him she didn't mean it, but the fact that he didn't try to stop her or change her mind showed the glaring truth of the meaningless tryst they'd shared.

Taking a deep breath, she straightened her spine and prepared her mind for the evening with Keith. Before going to see Ransom, she hadn't been sure she would forgive Keith, but she seriously considered doing so now.

Since Ransom didn't care enough to pursue a relationship with her, she'd give her boyfriend a chance to prove that he was not only a better man, but the type of man she needed.

Chapter Eight

Sophie parked her Jeep on the street in Midtown Atlanta and walked toward her mother's juice shop. The Juice Fox was the brainchild of her parents, long before juice bars became trendy. It was an Atlanta staple, known for selling juice and smoothie concoctions, with many of the ingredients sourced locally.

The bright green and yellow awning showed an illustrated fox on two legs, wearing a red polka dot dress, with hands on her hips in a pose reminiscent of the pinup models from years ago. The eye-catching sign beckoned to neighborhood residents and passersby using the busy street. The store was not only popular for its juices; stuffed foxes and other memorabilia sold in-store and online brought in a substantial side income.

Sophie entered the shop, bursting with red, green, and yellow designs, and filled with round tables where a scattered group of patrons chatted to each other or sat hunched over laptops and using the free Wi-Fi.

"Hey, you guys," she greeted two of the employees at the counter. One was at the juicer, pressing out an order for a customer. The other stopped to wave before continuing to bag the five glass bottles of fresh juice a man standing at the counter had just purchased.

Sophie's mother was not only conscientious about what went into her body, she was an advocate of protecting the Earth for future generations. The Juice Fox sold individual serving sizes of juice blends in plastic cups, but customers had the option to also purchase them in glass bottles, for a small one-time fee, which could then be refilled indefinitely at a discounted price.

Sophie found her mother in the back, sipping a red liquid from a tiny plastic taster cup. Two blenders, one half-filled with a green liquid and the other containing the reddish one in her cup, sat on the counter among cutting boards with various fruits and vegetables sliced and diced atop them. Apparently, her mother was working on a new recipe.

"Hi, honey!"

Dora Bradshaw's eyes danced the minute she saw Sophie, and she rushed over to give her daughter a tight squeeze. People often said they looked alike, but Sophie couldn't see the resemblance. She had amber skin, gray eyes, and dark hair. Her mother's white skin was very pale, she had blue eyes, and hair the color of her youth, courtesy of a box of Clairol Nice'n Easy in sun-kissed blonde.

Her mother stepped back and gave her a long look. She rubbed her hands up and down Sophie's bare arms. "You got a little tan while you were in the Bahamas."

"Yes, I did. I also received a surprise while I was there." Sophie crossed her arms.

"Oh?"

So that's how her mother was going to play it. The innocent role.

"Keith came to see me, and he told me *you* told him where I was."

"I had to."

"Why did you have to? You know I was there to get away, and you told him how to find me."

Sophie's father, Dr. Walter Bradshaw, came through the slightly ajar office door after he must have heard them talking. Over long dreadlocks he wore a black tam with red, yellow, and green stripes running its circumference, and was dressed casually in a T-shirt and jeans, which meant he didn't have plans to go into the office today.

One of the foremost authorities of black history and culture in the country, he taught African-American studies at Emory University, and wrote papers and traveled to do speeches on the subject. His age had begun to show by the smattering of gray hair in his neat circle beard, but he was still very fit. Her parents lived in town, and he rode his bike more often than not to the university or whenever he ran errands.

"Hey, Dad," Sophie greeted him, keeping an eye on her mother's guilty blush.

"What's going on?" her father asked, his heavy bass voice filling the space.

"The two of you encouraged me to take a trip on my own, and your wife ratted me out to Keith."

"I'm sure your mother meant well," Walter said, amusement in his voice.

Her mother shrugged. "He came by the house looking so pitiful. He practically begged me to tell him where you were, and how could I resist? He sounded sorry and seemed sincere."

"You could have at least warned me he was coming."

"That would have spoiled the surprise," her mother said, sounding reasonable.

Sophie huffed out a breath of exasperation. Her parents didn't know the whole story about Keith, and she didn't know yet if she'd tell them he'd cheated. All they knew was that they'd fought, and for now that was all she wanted anyone to know.

"So, what happened?" Her mother, ever the romantic, looked expectantly at Sophie.

She shrugged. "We talked for a long time. He's on probation and we'll see what happens."

"Your mother did the right thing, then," her father said.

"Of course you'd side with Mom," Sophie said dryly.

Their relationship was a model Sophie had admired for years, and one she hoped to replicate in her own life. Their affection and support of each other came from years of togetherness forged when their families initially disapproved of them falling in love. Her maternal grandparents were a conservative bunch who had expected their daughter to marry someone they'd already picked out for her. On her paternal side, they were a couple of intellectuals who expected her father to marry a woman with significantly more melanin.

Instead, her parents had fallen for each other after becoming lab partners in a class at university. They kept their relationship a secret for years until they finally came clean to their families, who initially didn't approve. Sophie never saw any of the disagreements, though. Apparently, her birth bridged the rift in the families, and she'd never felt unwanted by either side. If anything, she was showered with love and spoiled by affection on both sides of the family.

When he wasn't busy, her father came down to the shop to spend time with her mother, and he never took a meeting that lasted so late he couldn't walk her home after she closed up. On any given evening, they could be seen walking along the street, her father with the bike rolling beside him, and her mother hanging onto his arm. They were so cute.

"What are you working on?" Sophie asked, moving on from the conversation about her love life. She sniffed the green contents of the blender.

"Two possibilities today. The green one is a detox drink. I already have a name for the red one. It's called Watermelon Sunshine."

"Mmm, sounds delicious."

"I told your mother watermelon anything is a no-go," Walter said.

"Why, Dad?" Sophie picked up a watermelon slice and bit into it. Sweet and juicy.

"He thinks none of my black customers will buy it because of the whole watermelon thing." Her mother waved a hand dismissively.

"They won't," Walter insisted. "We've been married thirty-five years. I shouldn't have to explain that to you."

Dora sighed.

"Trust me, give the smoothie another name," Walter said. "Punch of Sunshine or something like that." He glanced at his watch. "Better get out of here. I have a dentist appointment. Sophie, will you be around later? I need a ride to pick up my car at the shop."

Her mother pursed her lips and shook her head as she went back to chopping ingredients.

"Seriously, Dad, you need to get rid of that car. Ronnie is going to ban you from the shop." Her father owned a blue eighties Volvo he refused to let go.

"Ronnie is going to do no such thing. That car is a classic, and as long as it still runs, I'm going to keep it on the road."

"It has over two hundred thousand miles on it," Sophie said.

"And your point is…?"

"He'll never listen," Dora said.

"She knows me so well." Walter pulled his wife in for a quick kiss and dropped one on Sophie's cheek. "I'll see you guys later. Sophie, don't forget me and my car," he said on the way out.

"Yeah, yeah."

Her mother wrinkled her nose. "Do you think he's right about the watermelon name?"

"Do you want to risk it?" Sophie asked.

"Punch of Sunshine it is," her mother said. She poured the mixture into a glass and handed it to Sophie.

She took a sip. "Mmm. Good. Sweet. Flavorful." She took another sip. "The ginger is a little strong, though. Hits me in the back of my throat on the way down."

"Noticed it, too." Her mother wrote a note to herself on a pad on the counter. "You okay, sweetie?"

"Sure."

Her mother tilted her head to the side. Her gaze held concern. "When you first came in, I thought you seemed a little off. It's not because of Keith, is it? I'm sorry, I shouldn't have butted in."

"He came to you. You didn't butt in." Sophie slipped her arm around her mother and squeezed. "I'm fine. Keith and I are fine."

If she seemed off, it had less to do with Keith and more to do with a certain civil attorney.

"Are you sure?"

"Positive. By the way, he invited me to a hoity-toity cocktail party his firm is having. And he invited me to join him in Chicago in a few weeks to meet his parents." He'd never done anything like that before.

"That's good, right?" her mother asked.

"It is." Keith was really kicking up his attention now that he recognized he could lose her.

"Then why don't you look more excited?"

Because she couldn't stop thinking about Ransom. A teeny tiny part of her had hoped he would reach out to her, but clearly she'd read more into their time together than was realistic. He'd offered her attention and affection when she needed it most, so it was only natural to get a little attached. She fully expected the heaviness of disappointment and regret in her stomach to disappear soon. Hopefully.

"I *am* excited. This is a new chapter for me and Keith, and…I'm going to hope for the best."

And pretend that every time she closed her eyes, she didn't see Ransom's face or remember the way he'd so expertly caressed each inch of her body until she shivered in his arms. Pretend she didn't long to see his roguish smile, twin dimples, and a muscular body that made her weak in the knees.

Chapter Nine

Ransom walked into the offices of Abraham, McKenzie & Wong on Monday morning, his strides long, steps sure. He'd spent the weekend poring over a case he hoped would soon be coming to an end. He rolled the taut muscles of his aching neck and shoulders, but he was certain the brief he'd stayed up until three in the morning to prepare would sway the judge in their favor and finally bring this case to a close.

Ransom was known in the world of civil litigation as The Shark, a nickname that encapsulated his personal work ethic and cutthroat reputation. He worked hard to win his cases, spending long hours combing through documents, motions, and answers to interrogatories with an unparalleled attention to detail. He was well respected by the junior associates working under him, and they all left his tutelage with a better understanding of the law and having grown as attorneys.

Sympathy tended to be stacked in favor of the plaintiffs, while his clients were often seen as greedy, self-indulgent corporations out to heap destruction on consumers and the world at large. The current case was no different, involving a manufacturer of a children's line of electronic toys whose owner he'd wooed over drinks at the Chicago Yacht Club, but he was certain the judge would rule in his favor at the hearing.

Walking down the hall to his office, he nodded and greeted the other attorneys diligent enough to show up as early as he did.

Near the end of the hall, he peeked into his assistant's office—one of the few members of the support staff who arrived early. She came early and left early, unless needed.

She looked up from searching a drawer in the large file cabinet in her office.

Lena was an older woman in her late forties or early fifties—he wasn't sure which—with reddish-brown skin. She had worked for the firm for many years and knew all the politicking behind the scenes, guarded a secret better than a first-time mother did a premature newborn, and at times he was absolutely certain she was clairvoyant, with her ability to anticipate his needs and foretell of changes coming down from the managing partners.

"Good morning," she said, adjusting her round-framed glasses, the colors of which changed from day to day, depending on which outfit she wore. Today the black frames matched her black pantsuit.

"Good morning. Anything for me today?"

By now he'd hoped to have received an invitation

to the annual cocktail party at founding partner Brit Wong's Atlanta home, an invitation that was the unofficial precursor to being voted in as a partner. Every day he checked his box, ever since he'd learned the invitations had been printed.

Lena pursed her lips and shook her head. "I'm sure it'll come soon," she said.

"No doubt about it, but I'm getting antsy," he confessed, something he'd only admit to her.

As he turned to leave, she said, "I saw Keith Wong in the office today."

"What's he doing here?"

Keith Wong was Brit's only son. An attorney himself, he was a legal administrator working out of the Atlanta office.

"Not sure. Probably reporting back to his father. Or…it might have something to do with you."

There she was, being clairvoyant again.

"You know that for sure, or are you guessing?"

"I'm pretty sure." She lifted a file out of the cabinet and shut the drawer. Lena walked over to her desk, dropped the file atop a stack of papers, and rested her fist on her hip. "It's good for you, bad for the lead attorney on the Creplar case."

Creplar, Inc. was an Atlanta-based software company being sued by ten of its top engineers, who alleged they were not adequately compensated for their designs. It was the Holy Grail of projects, representing thousands of billable hours thanks to mountains of paperwork, multiple depositions, and plaintiffs who not only refused to back down, they'd scoffed at earlier attempts to settle.

"I was told to call Wong's office when you arrived," Lena said in an ominous tone.

"Then go ahead and make that call. By the way, I'm meeting a potential client for coffee at two. Would you—"

"Make a reservation at the restaurant across the street? Already done."

Ransom went into his office and hung his jacket on the coatrack near the door. He sat down in his chair and tapped his fingers on the oak desk. If there was a problem on the Creplar case, as Lena suggested, the lead attorney could be on their way out and Ransom might have an opportunity to shine.

He signed off on letters Lena had drafted, printed, and placed on his desk. The call from upstairs didn't come until almost lunchtime, when he was five minutes into proofing a document prepared by one of the junior associates.

It was Mr. Wong's secretary. "Ransom, Mr. Wong would like to see you in his office, please."

Ransom stood right away and donned his suit jacket. On his way, he glanced into Lena's office, and she smiled and gave him the thumbs-up sign before ducking her head back to the paperwork in front of her.

Ransom exited on the top floor of the building, where Wong's secretary ushered him through with a smile. Since there weren't that many offices on this floor, it was very quiet. She knocked once on the double doors, pushed them open for him, and closed them after he walked through.

Ransom could only remember being in this office one other time in the eight years he'd worked at the firm, so everything seemed brand new to him. Heavy mahogany furniture covered in shiny leather dominated the décor, and the bookshelves lining the walls contained framed certificates, as well as law books.

Brit Wong sat behind his huge desk and looked up from a file he was reading. He motioned with his hand. "Ransom, come in, come in."

He was a slight man with a head full of grizzled hair and a black mustache and beard peppered with gray hairs. Years ago, he arrived in the United States from China and, because of a limited command of the English language, was forced to work menial jobs until he improved. Eventually he put himself through college and started the firm with Abraham and MacKenzie, both of whom he had outlived. Like many immigrants, he wanted a better life for himself and his family, and hoped to leave behind a legacy for his son, Keith, who happened to be seated across from his father in one of the maroon guest chairs, fiddling with his phone.

"Have a seat," Brit said, motioning to the chair beside his son.

"How are you doing, Ransom?" Keith greeted him.

Half Chinese and half Caucasian, he'd inherited many of his father's physical attributes, but was muscular and a bit taller. He'd passed the bar, but after practicing law for a few years, settled into the administrator position Brit handed to him.

"Doing well." Ransom crossed his legs and waited.

Brit closed the file in his hand. "I know we're all busy, so I won't waste your time," he said. After many years in the States, his accent had almost disappeared. He interlaced his fingers atop the desk. "Keith informed me of some not-so-good news on the Creplar case in Atlanta. I'm sure you're familiar with it, so I won't go into the details. It seems we're going to need someone to manage the negotiations until we arrive at a resolution. Attorney Belch is…ill—very ill, and will need to take a leave of absence for some time. We need someone who can jump in right away, which means not only taking over the management of the case, but spending quite a bit of time in Atlanta to make sure everything goes well. It's a huge undertaking, and I want you to make it your priority. We'll get support in place for you here, to help with your other cases. Would that be a problem?"

If by "ill," Brit meant Belch had fallen off the wagon, then they had a terrible problem indeed. Belch was one of the best damn lawyers in the entire firm. He'd been given a second chance and managed to stay sober for over three years, but apparently he'd just used up his second chance.

"Absolutely not a problem, sir. I'd be happy to take the lead."

"Thought so. You have family in Atlanta, don't you?"

"As a matter of fact, I do. My brother lives there with his wife and kids."

There was someone else who lived there, too. A certain flight attendant he'd thought about off and on over the past few weeks. He toyed with the idea of looking her up. Just to say hi. See how things were going with her and her lousy boyfriend.

"Great. You'll be able to spend some time with your family—but not too much, of course."

Although he smiled, Ransom knew Brit meant what he said.

"You have nothing to worry about. I'll make this my priority," Ransom assured him.

"I know you will. That's why I picked you when my son told me about the problem. Keith will brief you on the travel and housing details, and then I expect you to get completely up to speed so we can get this case closed out satisfactorily for our client." Brit nodded to his son. "I'll see you at dinner tonight."

The two younger men stood, and as they were walking out, Brit said, "Oh, Ransom, my secretary tells me she hasn't received your RSVP to the cocktail party yet. Are you planning to attend?"

His heart rate increased. "I haven't received an invitation."

Brit frowned. "That's a gross oversight. Clear your calendar. You're on the list. If you don't get your invitation within the next few days, contact my secretary."

"Yes, sir."

They walked out.

"I guess I'll be seeing you in Atlanta very soon," Keith said, as they rode down in the elevator.

"Looks like it."

"Do you have lunch plans? We can cover some of the details."

Ransom studied the younger man—five years younger, to be exact. He often thought of Keith as a spoiled rich kid, one who bragged too much and thought too highly of himself, with a questionable moral compass, even for an attorney. But he also suspected Keith admired him. He wouldn't be surprised if he had suggested to his father that Ransom replace Belch.

"I have a meeting at two, so we'll have to make it short."

"No problem. My girlfriend will be joining us, too, if you don't mind. She's visiting from Atlanta and I don't want to blow her off." He lowered his voice. "To be honest, I'm doing a bit of damage control. She gave me another chance, and for the past few weeks, I've been working my ass off trying to prove to her I'm a decent human being after I majorly screwed up."

"This sounds serious."

"It is. My player days are over."

"Good for you."

Ransom couldn't care less about Keith's relationship. He half listened, running through a list of tasks he had to complete in his head.

"Finally broke her down," Keith said, puffing out his chest.

Hating himself for being curious, Ransom asked, "How'd you manage that?"

"Lots of gifts and plenty of groveling. Women love some well-placed groveling." He laughed to himself.

"Glad it worked out for you." He knew very little about Keith, but what he did know was that he was a player. Ransom didn't even know Keith had a girlfriend, or had one that he needed to grovel to, so this was a bit of surprising news. Still, it was not his business. He already had plenty on his plate without wasting time at lunch when he had work to do.

"I'll see you around one-ish?" Keith called as they walked away from each other.

Ransom agreed with a wave of his hand and kept moving down the hall. He gave Lena the thumbs-up as he went by and left the door of his office open before sitting down to work.

Lena came in, glancing over her shoulder before she closed the door. She crossed her arms over her chest. "What did Wong want?"

Ransom gave her the details of the short conversation in Brit's office. She didn't appear the least bit surprised about Belch's fall from grace. "Good news. Brit confirmed I should get an invitation to the cocktail party."

Lena's eyes it up behind her glasses. "Yes!" She gave a reserved pump of her little fist. "That's wonderful."

Ransom leaned back in his chair, for the first time really accepting he'd received the invite. Oddly enough, the immediate rush he'd felt upstairs had dissipated rather quickly, and Lena appeared more excited than he was. Delayed reaction, no doubt. The invitation simply hadn't sunk in yet.

"Are you taking a date?" Lena asked.

"Going solo. Easier that way." Ransom wrote three names on a sticky note and handed it to Lena. "Pull these files. I need to get some work done before I have to waste an hour at lunch with Keith and his girlfriend."

Lena took the piece of paper. "Be careful," she said in a loud whisper.

Ransom frowned. "About what?"

She edged closer. "You know what. You're trying to make partner, and Keith can make the process difficult for you if he wants to."

"He won't."

"He might, and you don't want anything standing in your way. Especially not an overly indulged man-boy looking for a friend or mentor or whatever it is he wants from you. You know what happens when people get on his bad side. He makes life miserable for them. Remember Melinda in the New York office?"

"Melinda left because she screwed up," Ransom reminded her.

Lena raised an eyebrow in an expression that clearly said, *Oh really?* "That was the story circulated around the office, but she was on the partner track. Why would she make such heinous mistakes when in a couple of years, she could be a partner?"

Ransom had always wondered the same thing, but in this business, he'd seen all kinds of aberrations in human behavior. "Are you saying Keith had something to do with it?"

Lena leaned over the edge of the desk and spoke in a lower tone. "All I know is, one minute I heard he made advances to her and she turned him down, the next thing I heard, her expense reports contained fraudulent information and she was losing important files. Then she resigned."

Ransom sighed. "So you're saying I shouldn't piss off Keith if he makes advances on me?"

Lena jabbed a fist to her hip. "I'm saying play nice."

"I know how to play nice."

"Hm."

Lena walked out of the office, leaving Ransom alone, and he shook his head at her unnecessary warning.

Sometime later, in the process of conducting preliminary research on a case, he heard the sound of Keith's voice approaching the office. Ransom looked up from his paperwork, ready to address his colleague and his lady friend, when shock burst through his brain like an IED explosion.

"Ransom, this is Sophie Bradshaw. Sophie, this is Ransom Stewart, one of the best attorneys in our firm. He'll be joining us for lunch."

Ransom gripped the arms of the chair, assessing the startled but familiar features of the woman beside Keith. The heart-shaped face and golden skin had been emblazoned in his memory as permanently as a tattooed design. Her long, sable-colored hair hung in wavy tendrils to the tops of her plump, full breasts. Breasts that were just shy of a handful, which he'd squeezed with his hands, licked with his tongue, and nibbled on with his teeth.

He knew this woman. Every nook. Every cranny.

The very flavor of her skin.

Chapter Ten

Ransom didn't move. He didn't dare blink. Focused solely on her. He had no clue what to say. Their unexpected reunion must be some kind of joke. Or a trap. Or a test, certainly.

Sophie Bradshaw and Keith Wong?

Her wide gray eyes assessed him with uncertainty, trying to gauge whether he would mention that no introductions were necessary. They knew each other very well, after spending hours together talking and laughing and making ample use of the large bed in his waterfront suite.

Sophie recovered first. "Nice to meet you," she said, smiling weakly.

Registering that he'd been sitting and staring the entire time, Ransom shot to his feet. Normally, he extended a hand to guests, but he couldn't touch her. Too risky at the moment. The tumultuous emotions reeling out of control inside him might be revealed.

"Nice to meet you, too." His voice sounded tight and unnatural. He cleared his throat and stuck his hands in his pockets. "So this is your girlfriend," he said, pulling his gaze away from her before Keith noticed his odd behavior.

"My better half." Keith chuckled easily and slipped an arm around her waist, smiling like a self-satisfied cat who'd eaten the canary and drunk all the cream.

There was no air in the room. Ransom could hardly breathe. He pulled on the Windsor knot in his tie.

Keith looked at them both. "Are we ready to go?"

"Yes," Sophie said.

"Ready," Ransom croaked, though he felt anything but.

He should find an excuse to cancel lunch, but the word *no* couldn't be found in his vocabulary at the moment.

And he wanted to find out more about Sophie. What had she been up to since he saw her last?

****

A hum of conversation hovered over the packed room as the hostess escorted them to a square table.

Once seated, Sophie kept her eyes trained on the white tablecloth. The waiter took their drink orders, and she contemplated the vegetable soup, but doubted she'd eat much. The situation at hand made the prospect of food unappetizing. She'd never expected to run into Ransom again—with Keith, no less—and it wouldn't have happened if Keith hadn't surprised her by bringing her to the firm.

He looped an arm along the back of her chair,

completely unaware or uncaring of the silence and speaking enough for the three of them. In fact, he hadn't stopped talking practically since they left the building. She needed a break from his constant chattering to clear her head.

Fortunately, his phone rang.

"Hello?" Keith listened, and after a few clipped responses, he said, "Excuse me. I need to take care of a situation." He squeezed her thigh and left the table, the phone glued to his ear, talking in low tones.

Heavy silence settled between them before Ransom finally spoke. "Good to see you."

Sophie lifted her gaze. Like the first time she saw him, he looked ready for the cover of *GQ* with his perfectly coiffed hair, black suit, and skinny red tie. But like the last time she saw him, the warmth was completely gone from his eyes, leaving behind cold anger that seared to her soul.

"Same." She kept her voice cool, betraying nothing.

"Did you know?"

"Of course not."

"Bullshit."

"I didn't arrange this meeting," she said in a fierce whisper, appalled at the suggestion. "I had no idea you worked for the same firm, and definitely not that we'd see you today. I'm in shock. I only knew we were having lunch, and then he surprised me by bringing me to your office and introducing me to some of the attorneys."

He ran a hand down his face and let out a puff of air. "This can't be happening," he muttered. He leaned forward. The sleeves of the jacket pulled against his biceps when he moved in the chair, and

Sophie dragged her eyes away from the sight of those strong arms that had held her tight.

"So the guy you were talking about in the Bahamas, the one who hurt you and was trying to win you back, was Keith?"

"Yes." She didn't know what else to say, near tangible awkwardness at the table.

"He's an asshole."

She stared at him, but he appeared completely unrepentant. "He's changed. He's trying. He's not the same man he used to be."

He laughed dryly, tapping the table with a forefinger. "You hope."

His comment irritated her, as if she'd fallen short somehow by staying with Keith. "We have three years of history. It's called forgiveness and was not an easy decision to make."

A decision made even more difficult by the complication of their time in the Bahamas and the way Ransom made her feel. Seated across the table from him, when she never thought she'd see him again, was at once exhilarating and nerve-racking. She wished she could read his mind, but his face betrayed nothing.

Except for the surprise when he first glanced up and their eyes locked at the office, she had no idea how he felt. Even now he exuded rigid calm. While she felt vibrantly alive, her skin and every nerve sensitive and very aware of him.

"You forgave him? You said he slept with a waitress at your favorite restaurant, and you used me to get back at him."

Revenge sex. That was how she'd framed that night in her mind, but it had been more than revenge.

She'd been caught up in Ransom, his teasing words, and the excitement of his touch.

"You said he hurt you." His words sounded accusatory.

"He's changed."

"You think so?"

"What difference does it make to you? This is between me and Keith. Our relationship has nothing to do with you," she snapped.

A muscle in his jaw moved. Annoyance, perhaps. He muttered something unintelligible and looked away from her, swiping his thumb across his bottom lip, an act that made her nipples ache. His lips and thumb had paid an exorbitant amount of attention to her breasts.

Sophie swallowed. "I never thought I'd see you again," she said.

His fingers spread out and gripped the edge of the table. The same way they'd gripped her hips, as their bodies forged into one. Sophie glanced around for the waiter, wondering what was taking him so long with their drinks. She touched a hand to her dry throat.

"I guess fate had other plans," Ransom said.

Sophie focused on the tablecloth again. Maybe she should excuse herself until Keith returned. The bitterness coming from Ransom made her feel off-kilter and second-guess her decision to stay involved with Keith—something she'd already been conflicted about.

"He is different," she insisted, flicking her eyes to him again. She wanted to believe that. She'd seen the change in Keith. He was more attentive and considerate. Meeting here in Chicago had been his idea so they could spend time together.

"I guess we'll see." Clearly agitated, Ransom ran a hand through his hair. "You're right. You and Keith are none of my business."

The way he studied her increased the nervousness in the pit of her belly. "I'm glad you agree."

A muscle in his jaw ticked. "Did you tell anyone about what happened between us?" His voice had dropped low.

"No," she whispered.

"No one?"

"Who would I tell?"

"I don't know. A girlfriend or someone else close to you?" His thick brows lowered over his eyes, and a dash of discontent stained his voice.

Upon her return to the States, Sophie had wanted to tell someone, anyone, about her Bahamian fling, but in the end, she'd kept it to herself. The way he'd made her feel. The acts he'd perpetrated on her body.

"There was no one to tell. Did you tell anyone?" Her voice lowered, protective of their secret.

He sat back in the chair. "I mentioned it to a friend."

"What did you say?"

"That we fucked." He spoke crudely. Dismissively.

Sophie swallowed past the lump in her throat. "Because that's all it was." She waited with bated breath, hoping he'd deny the charge. The way they'd parted had left her reeling and confused, wondering if she'd misread the signals.

"Wasn't it? You were trying to get back at your boyfriend. Mission accomplished."

Sophie scanned the restaurant, searching for Keith. She wished he'd come back so she could avoid this painful conversation.

She ventured another look at Ransom. His face appeared hard and implacable.

"How long will you be working in Atlanta?" she asked, hoping the change in topic eased the tension.

He ran his fingers through his thick hair, and she curled her hands in her lap, recalling its texture. The softness. The lushness when she swept her fingers across his scalp.

"As long as it takes to close the case I'm taking over. Probably for a few months."

Months in the same city.

Conversations continued around them as diners chatted and laughed, but silence stretched between them again. Clumsy and ungainly, making a difficult situation even more so.

"You're not going to tell him, are you?" he asked.

"Do you want me to?" She held her breath again.

"What would be the point?"

Sophie nodded vigorously. "True. It was meaningless and would cause unnecessary problems."

Keith wouldn't like it if he found out she had slept with someone, especially someone at his firm.

"We'll just keep it a secret," she said, swallowing hard.

"Agreed." His mouth firmed.

The waiter finally arrived with the drink orders, and Sophie greedily swallowed the water to quench her parched throat. They didn't speak again until Keith returned to the table.

The two men talked mostly about the firm's business, steering clear of confidential details. Ransom hardly looked at her, but her gaze settled on him frequently, drinking in the strength of his features, the power beneath the jacket, and when he dared smile, even a little, the dimples that lined his cheeks.

Sophie marveled at the cruelty of the universe, amazed they should meet again in such a surprising way. Completely, and unexpectedly, by chance.

Chapter Eleven

Ransom was adept at compartmentalizing so he could focus on work, but right now he couldn't concentrate. It was early evening. Lena was gone and the office was quiet, and his thoughts constantly went back to Sophie. He needed to purge her from his mind.

He happened to know that Giles was working late on a case and Stephanie was out of town with a client. He figured Giles would be free—tonight, at least—and called his office.

"When are you leaving?" Ransom asked.

"Getting ready to head out."

"How about a game of racquetball?" He needed to expend some pent-up energy.

"Meet you in five minutes."

The racquetball court was located on the fifth floor. Before long, they'd changed into shorts, T-shirts, and tennis shoes, and engaged in a rigorous battle on the court with plenty of huffing and puffing. Each time, Ransom slammed the blue ball with all his might and Giles lunged mid court and dived into corners to keep up.

Eventually, Giles cursed loudly, slamming his racket to the floor with a loud clatter and shoving the goggles up onto his head. "What the hell is wrong with you?" he demanded, panting hard. "This isn't the racquetball Olympics. I thought you wanted to get in some exercise, not beat me to death with a little blue ball."

Ransom removed his goggles, too. "What's the matter, old man, can't keep up?"

Giles flung his arms in the air. "What are you trying to prove? Am I missing something?"

"No." Ransom huffed, the strenuous workout having taken his breath. He dropped back against the wall. "Truth?"

"Of course."

Ransom tossed his racket to the floor in frustration. "I had a bit of a surprise this afternoon."

"A case?" Giles, being the good friend he was, showed immediate concern.

"A woman," Ransom answered.

"Oh. Is it Lisa, or…?"

Ransom shook his head, laughing as he expelled a puff of air. He hadn't thought about Lisa in weeks, but she'd be an easier prospect to handle. "Remember the woman I told you I met in the Bahamas?"

Giles nodded. "The flight attendant."

"I saw her today. She's Keith Wong's girlfriend."

Giles's eyes widened. "Are you kidding me? You slept with Keith's girlfriend?"

"Of course I didn't know it at the time." Ransom

wiped sweat from his brow with his shirtsleeve.

Giles paced the floor, shaking his head in disbelief. "What are you going to do?"

"Nothing."

"But you like this woman?"

"There's something about her." He couldn't get her out of his mind, even after she rejected him.

"You barely know her, and if she's with Keith..."

"I was perfectly fine until I saw her again. I'd pretty much put her out of my mind, and then she shows up in the office, looking..." He ran frustrated fingers through his damp hair, and his words trailed off in disgust. *Looking beautiful.*

"You're sure it's not just the excitement of what happened in the Bahamas? If you haven't thought about her since then, what makes her so special all of a sudden? What is it about her that you like so much?"

"I didn't say I haven't thought about her since then." He'd purposely and deliberately not thought about her, refusing to dwell on what could have been. Every time she crept into his thoughts, he slammed a barrier in place. "To answer your questions, I like everything about her. She's beautiful and funny...and vibrant." That was the only way to describe her.

"And taken," Giles added.

"That didn't stop you with Stephanie," Ransom pointed out.

"Alexander wasn't the partner's son—one of the men you need to impress."

"I don't give a fuck about that," Ransom said.

"So now you don't care about the partnership? Because if that's what you're telling me, fine. Otherwise, you'll need to tread carefully."

"I don't know how to tread carefully." His first instinct was to stomp and growl and haul her away from Keith.

"She lives in Atlanta?"

Ransom nodded. "She does."

"Well…you'll be in Atlanta next week. Maybe you can tread not-so-carefully there," Giles said.

****

Keith sat on the bed watching her as she worked lotion into her hands. Sophie was staying at a hotel room near the airport to make flying out in the morning easy.

She hadn't expected him to invite himself to stay with her when she turned down his request to stay at his parents' house. Mostly she wanted time alone to think, but she hadn't been able to do much of that, spending almost every minute since she'd landed with Keith, being introduced to his coworkers and friends, and having dinner with his parents and, of course, lunch with Ransom, from which she still hadn't recovered.

Sophie sat on the side of the bed and worked lotion into her feet.

"You're awfully quiet tonight," Keith said.

"I have a lot on my mind. It's been a long day." Sophie pulled the sheet up to her waist and turned onto her side away from him. Settling into bed, she fluffed the pillow and closed her eyes, hoping that would be enough to make him leave her alone. "Good night."

He flicked off the lamp beside the bed. It was quiet for a while, and then he asked, "Are you asleep?"

"No," Sophie replied, though she was tempted to pretend she was.

"I'm glad you came to dinner with my parents tonight." His arm snaked around her waist.

She stiffened. "Keith…it's late." She pushed at his arm, but his grip only tightened. "I'm tired. I just want to go to sleep."

"How much longer are we going to do this?" Keith asked in a dull voice.

She didn't want to fight with him, but she had so much on her mind.

"How much longer, Sophie?" he asked again, his voice sounding harder this time.

"You want everything to be back to the way it was before, and it's not that easy for me. I need time."

"Time for what? How much longer are you going to punish me for something that I did in the past? You said you wanted to try again, but I don't see you putting forth the effort."

"I *am* putting forth the effort. I came all the way to Chicago, didn't I? I met your friends and your family because you asked me to."

"Are you saying you didn't want to meet them?"

"That's not what I said. You keep trying to pick a fight, and I don't want to fight with you. I'm tired and I want to go to sleep." She shut her eyes and hoped the conversation would be over and done with.

"You're testing me, aren't you? But I'm not going to fail the test. I meant it when I said I'm going to prove to you that I'm a different man. And I'm going to be the kind of man that you would want to be with. I just need you to be open and honest and give me a chance to prove myself to you. I know I was wrong before, and I'm trying to rectify what I've done in the past and be a better boyfriend."

"I know," Sophie said quietly.

He kissed her neck. "Come on, Sophie. How much longer are you going to make me wait? Haven't I been good?"

Closing her eyes, Sophie shut out his words. "Stop."

He kissed her neck. "Just a quickie," he murmured.

He pulled her onto her back and braced himself over her, kissing her fully on the mouth. His erection pressed into her stomach and she cringed internally, her hands coming up between them as she twisted her mouth away. "I'm not in the mood." She spoke softly, so as not to hurt his feelings.

Taking her wrists, Keith pinned them above her head with one hand and kissed her again, harder this time, and she tasted the desperate plea for acceptance and affection.

"Don't make me beg," he muttered.

She finally gave in. She'd put off sex with Keith long enough, but maybe intimacy with him was the antidote to forget about Ransom.

Forget him. Forget him.

Yet no matter how much she pleaded, her mind betrayed her. The more she tried to clear her thoughts of Ransom, the more she thought about him. Instead of seeing straight black hair, she saw the thick lushness of Ransom's dark tresses. Instead of dark brown eyes, sharp blue ones floated into her mind. She could even smell him. His scent was everywhere. All over her. The lines blurred about where she was and who she was with.

Her breathing fractured as she imagined Ransom

kissing his way down her chest, groaning as he pushed up the nightshirt and labored over her breasts. Then he moved down to her stomach.

His fingers slipped between her lower lips and played in the moisture between her thighs. "You're so wet," he muttered excitedly.

He pulled on a condom and entered her with ease, and Sophie gasped at the intrusion. She gripped his back, shuddering at the sensation of him filling her. His slow, hard strokes stole her breath. She moaned, tossing her head back as pleasurable sensations covered every surface of her skin.

He rubbed a finger across her clit, and a loud, breathless cry erupted from her throat at the same time a powerful orgasm tore through her body. Quivering, panting, she tightened her legs around his hips and buried her face in his damp neck.

When it was over, brown eyes looked down into her face. Out of breath, Keith smiled at her. "Wow. You came hard that time, didn't you?" He dropped kisses to her mouth and jaw. "Why'd you make me wait so long, hmm? Look how much you enjoyed that."

He rolled out of bed and headed to the bathroom.

Sophie groaned, biting her lower lip and yanking the sheet to her chin. She squeezed her eyes shut. Pity sex while thinking of another man. Something else to add to her list of transgressions.

Minutes later, Keith came back into the room and looped an arm around her waist. "I'm not giving up on us. I hope you aren't, either."

Sophie didn't answer, letting the words sit out there in the dark, wondering if it was already too late for them. Because it certainly was not a good sign to be lying in bed with one man…while thinking about another.

Chapter Twelve

The Atlanta offices of Abraham, MacKenzie & Wong were located smack-dab in the middle of prime real estate in the Midtown Business District, close to a MARTA train station and within walking distance of the Woodruff Arts Center, a not-for-profit dedicated to the promotion of the visual and performing arts. Shopping, offices, and art galleries dominated the commercial landscape, with outdoor recreation easily accessible in perhaps the city's most well-known greenspace, Piedmont Park.

One hundred attorneys occupied five floors and concentrated in civil, corporate, and family law. When Ransom entered the office on Monday morning, his office was already prepared and the assistant and paralegal assigned to him ready and waiting for the morning briefing. He gathered the rest of the attorneys, a total of ten, all dedicated to making sure the management of Creplar, Inc. did not settle—and if they did, it was the best settlement money could buy.

By Friday, he was already in the groove of the daily grind and not only had the hang of the Creplar case, but kept track of his cases in Chicago, too. The weekend meant poring over more documents to stay abreast of his work, but Ransom decided to do it from the short-term apartment the firm rented for him. Like his condo in Chicago, it boasted a modern design and was situated close to the firm—even closer, as it was within walking distance.

On Saturday, Ransom sat at the desk set up in the living room of the one-bedroom apartment, facing a window that looked out at the Midtown skyline. Files covered in sticky notes sat piled high on his desk, and the legal pad he wrote on contained detailed notes of angles he wanted the associates to follow up on. Despite all the work he had before him, passing cars and people traveling to and fro repeatedly drew his eyes from the legal pad and snagged his attention from the law journal he perused online.

He'd worked in other cities countless times, but there seemed to be so much activity taking place down there without him.

He sighed and pinched his nose.

Standing, he swiped the cell phone from the corner of his desk and searched for Sophie's number. He'd been here all week and been tempted to call her. He remembered she rode her bike with a cycling club on Saturdays.

For the sake of his sanity, he should leave her alone. She was off limits.

His thumb remained poised over her name, but instead of backing away from seeing her, he considered whether or not he should call first, or simply show up.

At the window he braced an arm above his head. It was early, not even eight yet. Maybe he could catch them before they left.

He dressed quickly, throwing on a pair of shorts and a T-shirt, and hoped he could rent a bike and buy the clothes he needed to ride at the shop.

Using GPS, he quickly found the juice shop with the bike store next to it. A brisk, short walk down the avenue brought him to the right location, and the area was easily marked by the group of ten cyclists hanging outside in the shared parking lot. He approached the group with a nod and morning greeting, searching for Sophie's face. When he didn't see her, he went into the store.

It was a fairly large facility, containing bikes, cycling clothing, and other gear.

Ransom greeted the young black man behind the counter.

"How can I help you today?" He was of average height, with a wiry body and a bald head.

"What time does the group pull out?"

"The Cycle Crew? Eight thirty."

"A friend of mine told me about them. Are you taking new members?"

"We're always interested in new members. Who told you about us?"

"Me." The soft voice came from behind him.

Ransom swung around to see Sophie only a few feet away. His appreciative gaze ran from the two braids on either side of her head, over the red and black biker outfit hugging her curves, and spent extra time on her sexy legs. A flash of memory came to him, of driving between those toned legs, of spreading them wide as he fucked her from behind and she panted her pleasure.

His shaft twitched in greeting.

"Hi." That was all he could think of to say.

"Hi."

Their conversation remained awkward, but without the ugliness from the lunch.

He stepped over to her and lowered his voice. "Sophie, last week—"

"Did I hear you correctly? You're going out with us today?"

She spoke at a normal volume, cutting him off on purpose, and he didn't know if he should be grateful or push through and force them to tackle their uncomfortable history.

"That's the plan," he said.

With her crimson helmet wedged between elbow and hip, her eyes flicked over his clothes. "You're going to need the works."

"Already ahead of you. My man here is going to help me out." He pointed a thumb at the clerk behind the counter.

"We leave in thirty minutes, so you'll have to be quick. Today we're riding the Cycle of Death. Think you can handle it?"

"Let me know what you think when you're trailing behind me," Ransom quipped, diving headfirst into the banter.

"Ooh, big words coming from a guy who hardly ever gets out to ride. We'll see how good you are in a little bit. Consider yourself lucky we're riding the short route today. Only thirty-five miles."

Hell, that was longer than he'd ridden in a long

time, but he'd be damned if he backed down now.

With a saucy grin, Sophie sauntered off, and he watched her progress all the way through the door. Outside, she greeted some of the members with hugs and others with kisses, and eventually joined them in pre-ride warmups.

Behind him, a throat cleared.

Ransom turned to find the young man smiling knowingly at him. "She's great, isn't she?"

He chuckled, a little embarrassed. "Yeah, she's something else."

"One of the nicest people I know, and the club's founder."

"Really?"

The young man nodded. "Other people have taken the lead since then. One of them is Eric, who you'll meet today, but if it wasn't for Sophie, we wouldn't have this club." He came around the counter. "Let me show you what we have."

They walked through the store, and pretty quickly Ransom purchased padded bike shorts, a lime-green jersey, a helmet, and gloves. Understanding the importance of hydrating and fueling his body while he rode, he went next door to The Juice Fox, where a young woman and Sophie's mother—he saw the resemblance right away—worked behind the counter.

She was busy ringing up orders from the bikers, and he purchased energy bars and two bottles of water—one he drank right away and the other he saved to slip into the holder on the bike. By the time he'd changed into his clothes, the bike he'd chosen to rent was ready, and he joined the group assembled outside.

Eric, the leader, asked Ransom and another

newbie to introduce themselves and tell about their riding experience. The members greeted them and welcomed them to the group, and then Eric took over, explaining the route and making sure everyone who wanted a ride map received one. Rest stops, places where they could rehydrate and replenish food supplies, were marked in green. By eight thirty-five, the group—which had grown to twenty-two—pulled out.

The Cycle of Death started on the main road and veered off into neighborhoods, along uneven terrain and around curves. The ride took approximately four hours, but it was one of the most exhilarating four hours Ransom had experienced in a long time. He stayed near the rear, keeping an average pace to maximize endurance, and kept a steady rhythm when going uphill—alternating between sitting and lifting off the saddle to stretch his muscles. Going downhill, he tucked his arms, elbows, and head, picking up speed as the headwind blew across his face.

The line of cyclists streamed past cars and buildings, stopping several times to replenish. At the last location, he and Sophie sat on a bench outside the rest stop, watching the other members stretch, drink water, and eat snacks.

"You never told me you started this club."

Sophie peeled a banana and extended it toward him. "How did you find out?"

Ransom broke off a piece. "The guy back at the bike shop told me."

She finished chewing a piece of the fruit. "I've been riding for years, thanks to my dad, who still rides a bike to work every day, by the way. Starting the group was a way for me to take advantage of the bike shop moving in next door and get like-minded people together. It grew bigger than I expected. There are over sixty of us, and about twenty ride out regularly."

She jumped up from the bench. "Come on, let's go before we get left behind."

The rest of the group had started getting on their bikes, gearing up for the final leg of the trip. Groaning, Ransom followed suit and climbed onto his bicycle. Seconds later they were on the road again, circling back to the shop at a leisurely pace. Sophie rode the last few miles alongside him, sometimes getting ahead, but always staying close.

When they were all crowded back into the parking lot, Sophie pulled off her helmet, and he almost reached up to smooth the fuzzy tendrils that framed her face. "Well, what do you think? Will you come back?" she asked.

"Definitely." His thighs and calves burned, and he was tired as hell, but right then and there, Ransom promised himself that he would do this more often. Get out more. Enjoy the elements and the freedom of just exercising and taking a few hours to think. During the ride, he'd even managed to work out the problem to one of his cases.

"Eric, we have another convert," she called over her shoulder.

The group leader smiled. "Welcome to the family," he said. "Considering you haven't ridden in a while, you kept up pretty well. Sophie, do you mind getting him signed up?"

"Not a problem." She looked at Ransom. "Follow me. The paperwork is in the back."

They went into the back office of the bike shop and she lifted a clipboard from the desk. "Fill in your contact information here." She pulled together a packet of papers and stacked them at the edge of the desk. "Mostly these are just waivers saying that you'll be responsible and adhere to all safety guidelines and rules of the road. You can read through them later and bring the signed acknowledgement with your membership fee when you come back next time."

Ransom finished filling in all his contact information and then handed her the clipboard. She scanned the page and then set it on the desk. "Now you're officially part of the group."

"Great."

They fell quiet, and he had the distinct impression she didn't want to leave any more than he wanted to.

"What made you decide to ride with us today? I'm surprised you're not holed up in your office, since it's your first week in Atlanta."

"I should be, but...I wanted to get out. See the sights." *See you.*

"Oh."

Quiet.

Sophie straightened the papers on the desk.

"You didn't give me a chance to explain about last week," Ransom said.

"There's nothing to explain. The meeting took us both by surprise and we reacted badly." She laughed, albeit a bit nervously. "Like you said, we both got what we wanted in the Bahamas, and...it's done. The fact that we ran into each other is a crazy coincidence. So...let's just leave the past in the past. Okay?"

"Right." He ignored the burning in his stomach, pushing through to ask a question he had no business asking. "You and Keith are definitely staying together?" His neck muscles stretched tight like bands of elastic.

"Yes."

He fought the urge to smash something.

Sophie took a deep breath and tucked her helmet under her arm. "I have to pick up my car at the mechanic shop, so I'll see you later," she said quietly.

They walked out to the parking lot together, and one of the other riders came rushing up with a grimace. "Hey, Sophie, I hate to cancel on you at the last minute, but I'm not going to be able to take you to get your car. I just got a call from the babysitter and she needs to leave right away. Can you catch a ride with someone else?"

"Oh. I—"

"I can take you," Ransom volunteered.

"Super! Thanks, pal. Sophie, I'm sorry. I'll make it up to you." The guy hurried away.

Sophie crossed her arms. "You don't have to take me. I can ask my mother."

"Your mother's working, and I don't mind." When she seemed to still hesitate, looking around the parking lot as if searching for an alternative ride, he added, "Buy me lunch. Consider it payback for taking you to the mechanic. For saving you again."

Just as he thought, the reminder elicited a small smile. "Saving me? I don't see a cape."

"Someone once told me not all heroes wear capes." He smiled at her. "Let me walk back to my apartment to get my car and I'll be back to pick you up."

"I'll wait for you at my mother's shop."

"See you in a few."

Chapter Thirteen

Riding in Ransom's SUV turned out to be a bad idea. Sophie knew she'd made a mistake as soon as she strapped into the seat. Sitting so close to him in a confined space evoked memories, and tiny pulses of need erupted over her skin. She crossed her arms over her chest.

"Where to?" he asked.

She gave him the address and he plugged it into the GPS.

They took off down the road, but a heavy silence hung over the car.

"I don't want things to be awkward between us," Sophie finally said.

"I don't, either."

"We're adults, and we had a fling. It should be no big deal. Surely we can be friends." She'd simply have to stop noticing the way the jersey molded to his chest or the black shorts wrapped tight around his powerful thighs.

He was silent for a while. The GPS indicated the next turn was a left, and he took it. "I suppose we could do that. Friends can ride their bikes together. Friends can drop each other off to pick up their car at the mechanic shop."

"Exactly." She felt as if a load had been lifted.

"Are you attending the cocktail party at the Wong home?" Ransom asked.

"Yes."

"I'll be there, too. It's supposed to be quite an event." He made another turn.

Sophie chewed on her lip. There was a question she wanted to ask, but hesitated. Finally, she could no longer hold it. "Are you taking anyone?"

"No."

She shouldn't be relieved. After all, she was going to be there with Keith. Nonetheless, she was relieved.

They didn't speak again until they pulled up at the mechanic shop. Sophie hopped down from the vehicle, and Ransom stayed outside while she went into the garage.

"Is Ronnie here?" she asked the guy behind the counter.

He picked up the phone and used the intercom. "Ronnie, you have a customer out front."

A few minutes later, a petite female with very short hair and deep chocolate skin came from the garage.

"Is my car ready?" Sophie asked.

"Yes, ma'am."

Sophie and her father, Walter, didn't trust anyone else to work on their vehicles. Ronnie was probably the best mechanic in the place. Walter had been bringing his car to this location for years, from back when Ronnie's father used to run the shop.

Ronnie typed into the computer and printed out an itemized receipt. "Your spark plugs need to be changed, but you're fine until the next tune-up." She handed the printout to Sophie.

"Thanks." Sophie signed and handed over her card. "By the way, would you please tell my dad to get rid of that Volvo?"

Ronnie laughed and swiped the card. "No way. Those babies are made to last. As long as he keeps up the maintenance, he's easily got a few more years on that car."

"Come on, Ronnie. That ancient thing drives me and Mom crazy. He needs another car."

Ronnie lifted her hands in surrender. "You're talking to the wrong person." She handed Sophie the sheet and she signed her name.

"I was really hoping to get you on my side."

"No way." Ronnie pulled the keys from the rack. "Here you go. See you next time."

Sophie waved goodbye and exited the building.

Ransom was waiting outside, back against the SUV and arms crossed, and she got a good look at him as she approached. The man was truly magnificent. The biker shorts emphasized his powerful thighs, and the fitted jersey molded to his sculpted chest and arms.

She took a deep breath. Whatever she felt would go away. It had to.

Please go away. Please.

"You ready for lunch?" Ransom asked.

Sophie nodded. "There's a Mexican place about a mile down the road."

"That's fine. I'll follow you."

They drove off in their respective cars, but even in

separate vehicles, Sophie felt this was a bad idea—a dangerous temptation. Her stomach twisted and turned in revolt. Being in Ransom's presence made her feel tingly and uber-aware of her surroundings. But she was the one who'd said they were adults and could handle a friendship, and she needed to act like it.

When they entered the restaurant, Ransom placed a hand at the small of her back. He dropped it almost immediately, but the fleeting touch jarred her insides and she stumbled mid-stride, which made him reach for her again, but Sophie jerked away.

"Are you all right?" Ransom asked, frowning.

"Mhmm. Missed my step."

On legs as sturdy as a wet sponge, Sophie trailed the hostess showing them to a booth near the window, and she fell onto the seat, willing her heart rate to slow down. Seconds later a server arrived and plopped down a bowl of chips and salsa in front of them.

They ordered quickly and then settled into another one of their awkward silences. They looked across at each other and laughed at the same time.

"We should relax, shouldn't we?" Sophie said.

"Yeah, we should."

She clasped her hands together on the table. "I'm curious about something…well, two things. Do you ever wear your earring? And the tattoos surprised me. That's quite a collection you have."

The tattoos were a variety of images, including the face of a lion on the outer biceps, and other pictures that were a combination of faces, places, and symbols.

Ransom rubbed a hand over the ink printed on his skin, which ended in a series of flames in the middle of his forearm. "All part of my rebellious youth."

"You? I can't believe it," Sophie said, eager to learn more.

"Believe it."

"Were you a bad boy at one time?" she teased. She remembered thinking on the plane that he had a certain edge to him under the preppy shirt-and-tie exterior.

"Let's just say I used to do a lot of foolish things when I was younger."

He didn't elaborate, and she didn't pry any further.

"Eventually you found your way," she pointed out.

"Eventually, but I drove my parents crazy with all the trouble I caused. The piercing I got in college, but the ink started in high school with some of my buddies, without our parents' permission, of course. I started off small, with these two arrows here." He pointed to the inside of his hard biceps. "By the time I'd graduated, I had a few tats. To be honest, half of these I added in the last three or four years."

"Really? That surprises me."

His mouth twisted up. "Why? Because I'm supposed to be a stuffy lawyer?"

Heat filled her cheeks. "I guess so, but that's silly, isn't it, to lump people who get tattoos into some kind of category?" She paused. "Why did you get so many recently?"

"I guess I had a moment of regret that I didn't get them before. Or I just needed…something to symbolize that I could still be as fearless as I was when I was younger." He said the last part slowly, in a more thoughtful tone.

"Not The Shark." Keith had told her about his nickname.

Ransom's eyebrows shot up in surprise, and he chuckled. "I'm afraid so."

He did that sexy thing again, where he rubbed a thumb along the edge of his bottom lip. She held her breath, lips parted as she watched him.

"You don't have any tattoos. Ever wanted to get one?" he asked.

"Who says I don't?"

"You don't."

The words were weighted. The implication was clear. He should know, because he knew every inch of her.

A tingling sensation settled between Sophie's thighs, and she squirmed in the seat to alleviate the sensation. "I thought about getting a tattoo once, but I never had the nerve to go through with it."

She glanced at a nearby table. A young brunette woman was staring at Ransom. When her eyes locked with Sophie's, she blushed and diverted her attention to her female companion in front of her.

The waitress arrived with two Coronas.

"You have an admirer at the table at three o'clock," Sophie said.

Ransom shifted his gaze and caught the woman looking. This time she was bolder. She didn't look away, letting her eyes linger on him.

"You should ask for her number."

He swung his head back to Sophie. "You think so?"

"Mhmm."

"Maybe I will." He tilted the bottle to his lips and made eye contact again with his admirer.

Sophie's stomach clenched until it hurt.

"If I'm lucky, maybe her friend would be

interested, too." He smirked this time, and looked Sophie dead in the eyes. "What do you think, pal?"

"I guess you'll have to see." She didn't like the direction of the conversation. She didn't even know why she'd suggested he get the woman's number. To prove she didn't care? To prove she and Ransom could be *friends*?

He twirled the beer bottle on the table and winked at the woman. The brunette winked in return and blew him a kiss.

What the hell?

Am I invisible?

"I could probably have them both tonight," Ransom said.

"You're a pig," Sophie said, voice tight.

"Me?" he said, cocking a brow. "I'm just taking what you said one step further, good buddy."

He was taunting her, but she had only been trying to establish a friendship between them. She needed to show him, and herself, that she didn't care about Ransom so much.

"You're being disgusting on purpose."

His jaw locked into a hard line. "And you're being ridiculous if you think I need you to tell me how and when to get phone numbers," he snapped. "I don't need you to coach me. I know how to get what I want from a woman."

Her heart jerked painfully. "You most certainly do."

"That wasn't a dig at you, it's a fact. I don't have a problem with us being friends, but I draw the line at you playing matchmaker."

The unexpected anger shut her down for a minute. Taking a deep breath, Sophie said, "Understood. I'll refrain from playing matchmaker. May I ask something of you, too?"

"Anything," he said slowly.

"Could you refrain from touching me? It's just a little...much." If they were going to do the friend thing, Sophie couldn't handle Ransom putting his hand at the small of her back—or anywhere else, for that matter.

He looked steadily at her. "I'll do my best."

At least they'd established ground rules for their friendship, but *I'll do my best* did not inspire confidence.

Chapter Fourteen

Ransom tapped his pen on the desk, reviewing the photos and report received from the investigator the firm hired for the Creplar case. A very interesting twist had developed in the past week. On a hunch, Ransom had asked the investigator to do some digging, and they discovered the lead plaintiff had invited a trio of hookers to a suite in Las Vegas—and the photos they uncovered would no doubt be of interest to his wife.

The lead investigator stood before him now. With a head full of brown hair, his average height and average clothes gave him an unremarkable appearance, allowing him to blend into the background of any environment and capture interesting acts of immoral and unethical behavior. He and his team had proved helpful over the years, and that was why the firm continued to hire him.

"Perfect. I had a gut feeling about this guy."

Ransom stuffed the photos back into the envelope. Now they had some leverage.

"Anything else?" The man stood but waited for further instructions.

"That'll be all for now. I'll share this with the rest of the team and we'll be in touch if we need anything else."

A knock came at the door. "Come in."

Sophie entered. "Oh. I'm sorry. You're busy."

The sight of Sophie, cheerful-looking in a yellow gingham dress and with her hair brushed away from her face, brightened the end of a long day but also made his chest tighten. She looked radiant, like sunshine. Perfect for the summer day.

"He's on his way out."

Taking his cue, the investigator inclined his head in greeting and left.

"I thought you'd be gone all week," Ransom said.

"I fly out again on Tuesday and I'll be gone for a week then," she explained.

"What are you doing here?" He assumed she must have come to see Keith and couldn't understand why she was standing in his office. His eyes dropped to the brown paper sack she carried with The Juice Fox name and logo printed on the side.

Sophie held up the bag. "I brought you a present, from my mom."

"Your mother sent me something?"

"We talked about you a little bit. She doesn't have many customers early on Saturday morning. The bike group keeps her busy, and she knows most of them now. She asked about you, and I told her who you worked for and that you're new to town, etcetera, etcetera."

He was tempted to ask if *etcetera, etcetera* included telling her mother about the Bahamas, but he knew better.

"She didn't get to speak to you this past Saturday, but wanted to welcome you properly to Atlanta."

Sophie set down the bag, and Ransom moved to sit beside it on the edge of the desk, one leg anchored to the floor.

"The red one is a new smoothie recipe she's still perfecting, which no one else but my father and I have tasted."

"I feel special."

"You should. The green one is a detox juice."

Ransom peeped into the bag and tapped the top of the glass bottle with the red juice in it. "I must be pretty special to get juice that no one else has."

"Keep in mind that my mother is a consummate salesperson, and she probably sees you as a potential goldmine. She's trying to impress you."

He grinned. "I'm impressed. Does she realize I won't be here for very long?"

"Trust me, she doesn't care. She included a card with instructions on how to order her products online."

Ransom folded his arms across his chest. "I see what you mean about her being a consummate salesperson."

She took a deep breath. "Well, that's all I came here for. I wanted to deliver this juice to you, say hi, and then…I'm off to see…"

Her voice trailed off, as if she couldn't say Keith's name in Ransom's presence. He didn't help her, either.

"Thank you. And thank your mother for me, too."

"You can thank her when you see her on Saturday. You are going to the next ride, aren't you?"

"I plan to. I enjoyed myself on Saturday, despite the fact that I had to soak in a warm bath afterward. I haven't really recovered. My legs are still sore."

He rubbed a hand up and down one thigh, and her gaze traveled the distance with him. She laughed shakily, licking her lips.

"The next one won't be as bad, I promise." Her voice sounded softer, huskier. "You hung in there like a trouper. I was impressed."

"That's all that matters."

Their eyes remained on each other, and quiet descended on the office, which seemed prone to occur whenever they were in the same place together, alone. As if they both wanted to say more, and since they couldn't, chose to remain silent.

This time the silence didn't feel awkward as in the past. It felt comfortable, as if they were getting accustomed to each other.

He touched the sleeve of her dress and let his fingers brush against the soft skin of her upper arm. She'd told him touching was off limits, but he couldn't resist this tiny gesture. "The colors you wear always look good on you. You smell good, too."

Friends could say that to each other, couldn't they?

"Thank you." Her cheeks filled with color. "I guess I'll see you when I get back."

Ransom hopped off the desk and grabbed her wrist as she attempted to walk away. He couldn't let her escape yet. Just a few more minutes.

She didn't move or pull away, staring up at him expectantly, waiting to hear what he had to say.

"Knock, knock—" Keith paused in the doorway,

the friendly smile dying on his face.

Ransom remained in place, but Sophie jumped back and snatched away her hand. Keith's eyes moved between the two of them, silently inquiring without speaking the words out loud.

Sophie broke the stiff silence in an overly cheerful voice. "Hi! I was just on my way to see you."

"Were you?" Keith ambled into the office and sent a sharp look in Ransom's direction. He tossed a set of files on the desk. "You probably want to take a look at these, as you're going over the documents for the Creplar case."

"Thanks," Ransom said stiffly.

Keith's gaze landed on the bag of juice. "What's this?"

"Mom sent those for Ransom, sort of a 'welcome to the city' gift."

"Why would your mother do that? Does she know him?" His brows arrowed down into a frown.

"He went on a ride with us on Saturday, and she saw him."

He looked at Ransom. "That's right. I forgot that you ride, too," he said slowly, thoughtfully. "But how did you happen to go to the same cycle club as Sophie?"

Ransom chose to answer simply but truthfully and put an end to the inquisition. "The cycle club meets at a bike shop not even half a mile from where I stay, so it was a no-brainer when I considered which one to join. I just pulled them up on my GPS."

"What a coincidence that club is the same one Sophie is a member of." Keith's smile was tight. He placed an arm around Sophie's waist, a move Ransom recognized as a man staking his claim.

Ransom curled his hands into fists while his insides railed against the territorial display.

"We better head to dinner. You ready to eat?" Keith asked Sophie.

"When you are," she replied.

"I'll see you later," he said to Ransom. "Enjoy the juice," he added, which sounded like a dig. Making it clear that was all Ransom was allowed to enjoy.

Keith took Sophie by the hand and led the way out. At the last second, she glanced over her shoulder. He couldn't read her expression, but his fisted hand tightened even more before she disappeared from view.

Ransom grabbed his phone, itching to destroy something. Anything.

He tightened his fingers around the device, desperate to smash it into the desk, but remembered how he'd ruined the last one. He took two deep breaths and carefully set it back on the piece of furniture.

Pressing his palms on the flat surface, he bowed his head, taking slow, calming breaths, and counted backward from ten.

Chapter Fifteen

Dinner had been a bust.

Sophie sat with her arms crossed, fuming on the passenger seat of Keith's car on the way to her apartment, and kept her eyes trained on the view passing by the window.

It seemed Atlanta never slept. As the most populous city in the state of Georgia, no matter the time of night or day of the week, cars filled the roadways with people traveling back and forth to one engagement or another at one of the many live music venues, trendy lounges, or restaurants.

Tonight they'd chosen to dine out, but the night was cut short after a fight about nothing. Maybe she had picked the fight. Maybe he did. They'd both been on edge, and when he'd asked testily if she wanted to tell him anything, she'd snapped back that if she wanted to tell him something, she wouldn't have any problem doing it.

When their soups arrived and there was nonexistent conversation at the table, Keith asked again if there was a problem. "Do you have to be so nice to the waitress?" she asked, taking perverse satisfaction in seeing his face color in anger.

"Why do you have to bring up old shit? Does it make you feel good to act like such a bitch?"

The meal ended right then, when she tossed her napkin on the table and demanded one of the passing servers tell their waitress to bring the check.

Keith pulled his car into the empty parking space outside of Sophie's apartment. The neighborhood contained a mix of small families and single people, with the majority of them having some link to the airline industry. The neighborhood was located south of the airport, which made for an easy commute to work.

Sophie stepped out of the car before Keith even turned off the ignition, and walked briskly through the breezeway to the door. She didn't want Keith to come in. She wanted to be alone.

She waited outside the door with her arms crossed. "You're still mad at me for the bitch comment?"

"When a woman's boyfriend calls her a bitch, I think she has a right to be upset."

"I didn't call you a bitch. I said you were acting like one."

"Thank you for the distinction, counselor. All is forgiven."

His nostrils flared. "You know what, I don't need this. I could…"

Sophie's shoulders stiffened painfully. "You could what?"

Blowing out a frustrated breath, he rubbed a hand

across his forehead. "Nothing. Forget I said anything."

"No, go ahead. Say what you're thinking," she goaded him.

"I'm not going to be pulled into an argument with you," Keith said through gritted teeth, "because that's obviously what you want."

"And what do you want?"

His eyes flashed with irritation. "You want to know what I want? I want *you* to understand that I'm a good catch. There are a lot of women who would be happy to be in your place."

"Well, there are a lot of men who'd love to be in yours," Sophie snapped back.

His eyes widened. Tense silence settled between them.

Tilting his head, Keith narrowed his eyes on her. "Are you trying to tell me something?"

Heart racing, Sophie realized she'd said too much, but in that moment she was angry and hurt, and oh, how she wanted to rub his nose in her tryst with Ransom. Tell him how he'd given her multiple orgasms. Tell him how he'd done such a comprehensive exploration of her body with his hands and mouth that phantom sensations flitted across her skin on occasion.

But she didn't say any of that.

"Are *you* trying to tell me something?" she shot back.

Keith didn't speak for a while. He just watched her, and she held his gaze.

"I guess I'm not coming in tonight."

"That would be correct." She imagined her rigid smile probably looked more like a sneer.

He sighed heavily and cursed under his breath.

Sophie waited for him to walk away, but he didn't. Instead, he bent his head for a goodnight kiss, and she gave him her cheek. In response, he grasped her chin in his hand and pressed his mouth against hers. She refused to kiss him back, keeping her lips pressed together until he finally gave up and stepped back.

"I'll call you tomorrow," he said.

"Fine."

They stared at each other for a few seconds longer before he spun on his heels and walked away.

Sophie stomped into the apartment and slammed the door. She chucked her shoes in the corner and flipped on the lights in the living room before tossing her purse on the coffee table and collapsing on the sofa.

The apartment was an eclectic mix of mismatched furniture—consisting of old and new, prints and stripes—that managed to work. Some pieces were modern, like the amethyst-and-olive striped sofa she was lying on, while others were flea market finds or unique pieces she'd fallen in love with on her travels—like the slatted table bench she used as a coffee table, purchased on a trip to West Africa with her father.

Sophie turned toward her purse, itching to make a phone call but knowing she shouldn't. Maybe that was why she'd been "acting like a bitch" tonight. She'd felt off ever since the visit to the law firm and seeing Ransom.

She stared long and hard at the purse.

"Screw it," she muttered.

She took out her phone and dialed Ransom's number. Even as it rang, her belly trembled. She shouldn't be doing this.

But why not? They were just going to talk.

"Hey."

His warm voice caressed her ear. That was the only way to describe the effect. It soothed her ruffled emotions, and she settled on her side against the arm of the sofa with her shoulder cushioned by pillows, half curling into the sound.

"Hey, yourself. I was calling to see how you liked the juices." She cringed at the lame reason she'd pulled out of her ass for calling him. He probably hadn't even tried either one yet.

"Are you part of your mother's quality control team?"

She appreciated his teasing tone.

"Something like that," she answered with a smile, staring at the window. The sheer curtains were pulled to the sides and the blinds were open a crack so she could see the streetlights outside.

She heard him moving around, and the clanging of pots.

"I'm happy to report that I liked them both. The red one is really, really good. The detox drink is good, too. I tasted celery and mint in it."

"You have a very discerning palate."

"So I've been told."

She heard the clang of pots again and frowned. "What are you doing?"

"Nothing much."

"I hear a lot of noise."

He was silent for a few seconds. "I'm cooking."

"At this hour?"

"I do that sometimes. I get the urge and I have to do it. Helps me think."

"I had no idea you even cooked."

"A little bit. Nothing fancy."

"You'll have to cook for me one day." She bit her lip. She couldn't believe she'd just invited herself over to his house for a meal.

"I've never done an entire vegetarian meal. Cooking for you would be a challenge."

"Are you saying you're not up for it?" she asked, a playful lilt to her voice.

"I'm always up for a challenge." No doubt that was a perfectly innocent remark, but it sounded sexual.

Sophie eased a hand under the hem of her dress and caressed her outer thigh. The skin there was so sensitive.

"That I believe," she said. "What are you making tonight?"

"Steak with mushrooms and a red wine sauce."

"I thought you said nothing fancy. That dish sounds complicated."

"Not at all. The steak goes on the grill, and the sauce will cook down on its own, getting to a thick consistency after about twenty minutes."

"What are the sides?"

"Cauliflower gratin, and grilled kale and radicchio with a drizzle of a light balsamic glaze."

Sophie's eyebrows rose. "You're cooking your ass off. Sounds delicious."

And sexy. She conjured an image of him with his sleeves rolled up in the kitchen, while a pot simmering on the stove disbursed the fragrant aroma of the sauce. The muscles in his forearms would ripple as he chopped the mushrooms and sliced the kale and radicchio. She knew he'd be all into the task, concentrating as he worked, his jaw tight as he focused.

Her hand inched toward the edge of her panties.

"If you ate meat, I could save you some," Ransom said.

"The sides sound good. I could eat those."

She brushed her fingers between her legs and stifled a gasp. If she was this turned during a perfectly normal, prosaic conversation about food, she couldn't imagine what would happen if they actually had phone sex.

"You sound odd," Ransom said.

"I'm fine."

She did sound odd. Her voice had dropped lower and contained just a hint of breathlessness. Maybe she could rub one out, a quickie, while talking to him. Sophie twisted restlessly with the phone attached to her ear and turned onto her stomach. She rubbed her sensitive nipples into the cushion and closed her eyes, squeezed a hand between the sofa and her hips, and touched herself again.

A needy little whimper escaped.

Her eyes flew open and she became very still. She knew he'd heard her because he stopped moving around. His end of the line had gone completely quiet.

"Sophie?" he said, voice low.

Her cheeks burned with embarrassment and she cringed, pressing her face into one of the pillows to hide, even though he couldn't see her. "Yes?"

"What are you doing?"

"Nothing."

"Are you—"

"I should go. I have stuff to do."

"Wait a minute, I—"

"Bye." Sophie hung up.

Right away the phone rang again. She declined the call.

It rang again. She declined again.

Sophie stared at the screen and waited, body tense, breath locked in her lungs.

After a few minutes she realized he wouldn't call back, and relaxed.

She closed her eyes and sighed in frustration. So much for being friends. She couldn't even talk to him on the phone without getting aroused.

Chapter Sixteen

A ringing phone was the last thing Ransom wanted to hear, but the caller was persistent. He knew because the calls came close together, and despite not answering the first two times it rang, the phone now rang for a third time.

He rolled over and snatched up the phone. "What?" he barked into the mouthpiece.

"It's worse than I thought."

The sound of Sophie's voice soothed and calmed him, but he was in no condition to talk. He had a runny nose, sinus headache, and a bad attitude because postnasal drip had kept him awake most of the night.

"Sophie, I—"

"I know, you're sick. That's why you missed the ride this morning and why you didn't show up for work yesterday. That's why I'm here."

For the past three weeks, he'd joined the Cycle

Crew on their rides, enjoying the time with Sophie, the rest of the group, and the freedom of the open road. But three days ago he fell ill. He hardly ever got sick and thought he'd caught a summer cold, practically unheard of as far as his immune system was concerned. He went immediately to the doctor and learned he did not, in fact, have a cold, but was diagnosed with a sinus infection.

"What do you mean you're here?" He rolled onto his back amid the rumpled sheets and pillows.

"I'm in the lobby and coming up, but I wanted to call first. See how polite I'm being?"

Ransom found himself smiling a little. "You should have called before you came over."

"Where's the fun in that? Tell me your apartment number."

"Eleven-oh-one."

"I'll be up in a little bit, and you better open the door."

As if he wouldn't.

Ransom lay in bed for another full minute, giving himself a pep talk to encourage movement. Groaning loudly, he rolled his achy body to the side of bed and nudged the wicker basket half filled with facial tissues out of the way of his feet.

Coughs caused by postnasal drip racked his body and kept his butt on the mattress. "Get up," he muttered to himself. He blew his nose and tossed the tissue in the wastebasket.

Passing by the mirror on the dresser, Ransom did a double take. He actually looked worse than he felt. He hadn't shaved in days, so a healthy layer of stubble covered his cheeks and chin. The wrinkles in his sweatpants had wrinkles, and so did the gray sleeveless undershirt. His red nose rivaled Rudolph the Reindeer's, and strands of hair stuck up in all directions, as if he'd been electrocuted.

He patted down his messy hair and then, too tired to continue, dropped his arm. Screw it. She'd just have to see him at his worst.

Sophie knocked before he made it to the door, but he swung it open, and she stood on the other side, balancing a paper sack on her hip, a neat, curly bun on top of her head. Red, orange, and green bangles circled her wrists and the matching earrings hung in her ears. The bubblegum-colored lipstick she favored tinted her smiling lips and gave them a moist appearance.

She was radiant, like a ray of sunshine breaking through storm clouds. The sight of her gave a small boost to his inert spirits.

"You look like crap," she said.

"Thank you." Ransom sniffed and rubbed a hand under his nose.

"Are you going to let me in, or...?" She cocked a brow.

He stepped aside, and she marched across the threshold in wedge sandals and a pair of skinny jeans that hugged her hips and bottom. He might be sick, but he wasn't blind.

"Go back to bed. I'll bring you some chicken soup," she said over her shoulder on the way to the kitchen.

"You're going to cook chicken?" He stood in the middle of the living room, confused, but appreciative of her consideration. He couldn't remember the last time anyone had taken the time to offer him such care. Even Lisa, whom he'd dated for a couple of years, never did anything like this. Between the distance and her work schedule, she couldn't take the time to be so nurturing.

Sophie paused and wrinkled her nose at him. "Cook chicken? Don't be absurd." She reached into the paper bag and pulled out a glass jar. "From the local grocer. Now go back to bed."

She deposited the container back into the bag and made a shooing motion with her hand before continuing her march to the kitchen. Ransom couldn't see the activity in there, but heard her moving around, opening and closing cabinets, and sliding open drawers. The smile threatening to make an appearance since she'd arrived finally broke free and spread across his face.

He returned to the bedroom and grabbed a tissue just in time for a sneeze that landed with such force, it threatened to tear his head off. He gladly fell into bed and dragged the covers up to his waist.

The smell of soup wafted through the open door of the bedroom, reminding him he hadn't eaten much, except for a piece of buttered toast first thing in the morning. He tapped his fingers on the mattress impatiently, his stomach rumbling in anticipation of a decent meal.

When Sophie finally came in carrying a steaming white bowl filled with the fragrant soup, the scent of chicken and fresh vegetables filled the bedroom. He almost leapt on her as she walked carefully across the carpet, balancing the bowl in both hands.

Ransom sat up against the headboard and she handed off the meal.

"I couldn't find your bed tray. Where is it?" she asked.

"I don't have one."

The rising steam brought his congested nose temporary relief. He wolfed down the broth, despite the bland taste. It needed more salt, and he would have added more thyme and celery for extra flavor. While he ate, Sophie took the wicker basket from the room. When she returned, it was empty, and she carried a small plate with some kind of green, tubelike food on it.

"How is it?" she asked when she came back in.

"Okay." He continued eating, barely stopping long enough to take a breath. "What are you eating?"

"Stuffed grape leaves. Want some?" She sliced one with her fork.

"Not unless they're stuffed with chicken."

"You don't know what you're missing," she said in a singsong voice.

"Pretty sure I do," he sang back.

She giggled, a sound he knew he'd never get tired of and wished he could hear more often. The thought jolted him. With the Creplar case wrapping up, he'd be moving back to Chicago soon.

Ransom tilted the bowl to his mouth, draining the last of the liquid.

Sophie looked amused. "There's more, you know. Do you want me to get you some?"

"Do you mind?"

"No, I don't mind. That's why I'm here." She left the room with both their dishes.

Ransom's head fell back against the headboard. He massaged the area between his eyes, vacillating between happiness she had come and frustration at having to keep from touching her.

Being friends with a woman he'd slept with was

pure bullshit.

A few minutes later she reentered the room with another heaping bowl of soup. "Here you go."

He gladly took it and dug in.

"What medicine are you taking?"

He inclined his head toward the nightstand and the collection of prescription pills. "I think it's time for another dose, actually."

Sophie checked the labels and tossed some tablets in her hand. She handed him the glass of water on the nightstand, and Ransom swallowed the pills and went back to eating. He ate the entire second bowl while Sophie puttered around the room. She fluffed his pillows and picked up clothes discarded on the floor, tossing them in the hamper.

When he finished eating, Ransom set the bowl on the nightstand. Time to ask the question uppermost in his mind since her arrival. "Why are you here?"

She paused in the midst of tucking the sheets at the foot of the bed. She seemed uncertain on how to answer the question at first. "Because men are the biggest babies when they're sick. And..." Her eyes softened. "You need someone to look after you because you're alone. I guess I'm it."

"So you feel sorry for me?"

"Something like that." She walked to the side of the bed and peeped at the bowl. "Finished, I see."

He caught her wrist. It had been hard, very hard not to touch her when she was so close. The type of restraint needed to resist simply didn't exist. Certainly didn't exist within him.

She tried to tug away, but his fingers tightened around her wrist. "Lie down with me."

Her eyes widened. "What? No."

"What else do you have to do?"

"I have to wash the dishes."

"Wash them later."

His thumb ran back and forth over the slender bones beneath her skin.

"You need to rest."

She was right. The simple act of eating combined with the meds kicking in sucked his energy and made him lethargic, but he wanted her at his side.

"Rest with me." Surely she wouldn't make him beg.

"It's not a good idea." Her eyes pleaded with him to understand and let go.

He didn't care about bad ideas or good ideas, right decisions or wrong decisions. She'd come here into his personal space, and he craved closer contact.

"I promise I won't try anything." She had him all out of sorts. He was supposed to be a shark, but Sophie made him as weak and nonthreatening as a damn guppy.

Her shoulders lowered as she weakened. "Just for a few minutes," she whispered.

He made room for her on the bed, and she lay down beside him. Ransom pulled her close, nudging his face into her jasmine-scented neck.

A sense of peace overcame him. As if he was...home.

It took a few minutes, but slowly her tense body relaxed, and she softened against him. Her supple breasts brushed right below his chin, and, unable to resist, he kissed the twin mounds, prompting her to release a shaky breath through her nose. He caressed her back, moving slowly down to the base of her spine and spanning the width of her sweet ass. That elicited a whimper. She threw one leg over his and did a slow, brief grind against his pelvis.

He was hard and aching, but she felt incredible. Wedged between her thighs, her warm, soft body enveloped in his arms, was the only place he wanted to be. To hell with the fact that she belonged to another man. Right now, in this moment, she belonged to him.

Sophie's fingers feathered through his hair and massaged his scalp. Brushing a thumb across his brow, she aided in relieving the sinus pressure there. He rested his head against the pillow of her bosom as she continued to gently stroke his hair. Under the gentleness of her calming caress, his eyes fluttered closed and his breathing slowed down.

"Thank you," he murmured.

Before he fell into a deep sleep, he could almost swear he felt her kiss his forehead.

****

Ransom awoke hours later, still feeling stuffy and achy, but the antibiotics and decongestant must finally be taking root in his body, because he didn't feel as bad as he had earlier. Sophie was no longer in bed with him, but her scent remained on the pillow. Even through a congested nose, he couldn't miss the fragrance of jasmine she left behind.

He listened for a minute to the quiet apartment. Had she already gone home?

With no sound to be heard, he set his feet on the floor and went to use the bathroom. When he finished, he blew his nose and slipped his feet into fleece-lined slippers.

He found Sophie in the living room, sitting at his desk with her eyes glued to the computer screen. He came closer to see what held her so engrossed she didn't notice he'd entered the room. Then he saw what she was reading.

"What the hell are you doing?" Ransom demanded.

She jumped, clutching her chest. "I—"

Angry at the invasion of privacy, he snapped, "You had no business snooping in my computer."

"I wasn't snooping. I wanted to log into the system at work, and the Word document was open and—"

"And you started reading, which you had no right to do. It's confidential."

"What's the big deal?"

"You invaded my privacy."

She stood, staring at him in open-mouthed shock. "I'm sorry, I didn't mean to, but your restaurant plan sounds amazing. It is your plan, isn't it?"

Her flattery did nothing to assuage his anger. "Yes," he said tightly.

"The portabello mushroom burger with caramelized onions and roasted peppers—oh my, it sounds delicious."

He hesitated. She'd been his inspiration for adding the vegetarian items, and the idea for the mushroom burger had come to him out of the blue. Each time he created a menu item in his head, he wrote down the list of ingredients and a full description. He even had a mock-up of the menu, which he sometimes revised. With a farm-to-table restaurant concept, the menu would change seasonally. A few days ago he'd opened that document, for the first time in weeks, and typed new ideas he planned to test.

"Vegetable lasagna is one of my favorite things, and that sounds good, too."

"You're just saying that," Ransom muttered.

"No, I'm not," Sophie insisted.

She sounded genuine, and if there was one thing he knew about Sophie, she was genuine.

Ransom scrubbed a hand through his hair. "Those plans don't mean anything."

Her eyes widened, as if he was crazy. "I don't mean to pry, but help me understand why not. They're very detailed."

"Cooking is a hobby. That's it. Something to pass the time."

The more they talked, the more irritated he became. He guarded this part of his life with aggressive tenacity. He had notebooks filled with ideas and recipes, demonstrating how his ideas evolved over the years. Most days his tools of preference were his laptop and the recorder app on his phone, but he was under no illusions about the viability of the restaurant business.

He snapped the laptop closed. "This conversation is over."

Chapter Seventeen

Why are you here?

That was the question he'd asked her. Sophie came because yesterday she went to meet Keith for dinner, hoping for a glimpse of Ransom. Nine times out of ten, when she was with her boyfriend, she was thinking about Ransom. Was it right? No, and she certainly wasn't proud of her thoughts, but she couldn't escape them.

The office manager at the firm had told Sophie that Ransom was out sick. Then this morning he didn't show up at the bike shop. She never completed the route, doubling back so she could run off and get supplies for him.

She'd worried about him, so it only made sense that she was disturbed to hear him dismiss his talent, like someone severing the spoiled spot from an apple and tossing it away.

"Forget I said anything." Sophie left him in the

living room. She returned to the kitchen and ran water in the sink to wash the dishes. She had no business being there, intruding on his life and space.

"I'm sorry." He stood in the open entrance between the kitchen and living room.

Her hands stilled in the soapy water, and she glanced over at him. He looked ill but adorably scruffy. His hair was a mess, and he needed to shave, but she had to admit that having his hair-roughened face against her breasts had evoked an involuntary need in her loins. The rumpled sleeveless shirt and sweats only added to his appeal, showing off his muscular tattooed arm and hinting at his firm thighs.

"Don't worry about it," she said.

"My ideas about the restaurant are private," he explained.

"Why?"

"First of all, I don't know if I'm any good. I'm not a professionally trained chef, and…opening a restaurant is a risky venture," he mumbled. Resting a hip against the counter, he studied her.

She didn't know this person. The confident lawyer was vastly different from the hesitant chef.

"You don't have to do it alone. I'm sure you know that restaurants often have multiple investors. You could even start with a small place and maybe one day grow into multiple locations." She dried her hands on a towel. "If you ever want to test your vegetarian recipes, I'll be your guinea pig." Her weak smile drew one from him, too. Encouraged by the softening of his attitude, she asked, "Do you ever cook for anyone else?"

"Not anymore."

"Why not? You have to get other opinions to

know if you're any good."

"Cooking takes time and energy, Sophie." He spoke to her as if speaking to a child.

She rolled her eyes. "Not that much time and energy, and actually *doing something* will get the ideas off paper and make it more real. Your ideas will go from concept to reality."

He rubbed his forehead. "I don't know."

"How will you know if you're any good if you're the only one eating your food?"

He chuckled. "I've had other people eat my food."

"You just said—"

"Not nowadays, but in the past. In college, that's how I paid my expenses. I worked part-time in the dining hall at first, but then I started cooking in my apartment every so often. It got to the point where friends would chip in five, ten bucks each and I'd get all the groceries and cook several nights a week. They even left me tips."

Her mouth fell open. "Are you serious?"

He nodded with a laugh. "I made so much off of tips and cooking, I was able to quit my job at the dining hall." He shrugged.

Sophie marched over and thumped his arm.

"Ow. I'm sick." He furrowed his brow at her and rubbed the spot she hit.

"What is wrong with you? You're obviously an excellent cook. Why won't you let people enjoy your food?"

He shrugged again. "I don't know how to explain it. I have a burning desire to create, even if no one else tastes it."

He seemed genuinely perplexed by the dilemma, but she understood. "Passion," she said quietly.

He nodded. "Yeah. Passion."

They smiled at each other.

"Take the leap," she said.

Hesitation surfaced in his eyes, but Sophie suspected it wasn't just about failure, because he faced the possibility of failure every time he took on a new client. With millions of dollars at stake and clients depending on his legal acumen, he carried a heavy load every day he worked. What she saw manifested in his eyes was much more.

"What's holding you back?"

He rubbed his neck. "Remember I told you I did a lot of dumb shit when I was younger?"

She nodded.

"I was into everything stupid a teenaged boy could get into. Smoking pot. Vandalism. Joyriding. You name it, I did it. I got into trouble often, but always got let off the hook because of my family name. People in the community loved and respected my parents, so it was perplexing to have a son turn out to be such a screw-up." He braced his arms on the counter behind him. "There were plenty of people who thought I was a lost cause, that I would end up dead or in jail because of my foolish behavior. I was basically told, on more than one occasion, that I wasn't shit and would never be shit."

His jaw hardened, and her heart broke a little. She sensed the pain he must have experienced, the self-doubt as he continued in the same destructive behavior, essentially living up to the negative comments that had been levied at him. She didn't think he'd speak on the topic anymore, but he continued.

"One of my teachers, Mr. Lang, told me I was too

smart to be throwing my life away. He had a brother who owned a restaurant and convinced him to hire me—washing dishes, of all things—and working at that restaurant kept my ass out of trouble. Mind you, I hated it at first. No teenager wants to spend his evenings and weekends washing dishes."

"Of course not, but having the job obviously helped."

"Redirected my energy," he confirmed. "My past created problems when I wanted to go into law. You can become a lawyer with a criminal background, but they make you jump through some serious hoops. Fortunately, I did all of my dirt as a juvenile."

She looked down at her hands, trying to form the right words to encourage him. Heaven knew she'd made mistakes over the years with her decision-making, so she didn't want to come off as lecturing. "I can't tell you what to do, but you should really—"

"Sophie, I'm one of the top attorneys at my firm."

"I understand, and you should be proud of your accomplishments. But who says you have to be restricted to one career? You've obviously been working on your idea."

"It's a silly hobby that won't amount to anything."

"Aren't you the person who just told me he used his cooking skills in college to feed his friends and pay his expenses?"

He laughed. Goodness, he was gorgeous. All dimples and white teeth.

"Touché, but that was years ago. I don't have time to dedicate to cooking. Not like I used to. It's more sporadic now, when I have time. If I have time."

"Make time."

"You're very bossy, you know that?" He pursed

his lips for several seconds. "I'll think about it. One day I'll cook and you can come over to eat."

"I can't wait." She bounced excitedly, honored to be privy to this side of his life, a side hidden from others.

Ransom stared at her, and some phantom emotion flashed across his face. Their eyes remained on each other, and the moment seemed frozen in time. Her pulse pummeled her wrist.

He walked toward her, and not knowing what else to do, Sophie stayed in place, afraid to break the spell. "There's no one else like you, is there?" He studied her face, eyes scouring her features, then moved abruptly away. "Time for another dose of antibiotics," he said, heading toward the living room.

Her heart constricted painfully. She should have said something or given a hint of how she was feeling. Admitted there was no one else like him, either, and that she thought about him constantly—an indecent amount.

But she'd promised Keith she'd work on their relationship, and meant to do it. Keith was a sure thing. Ransom wasn't. When his assignment in Atlanta was over, he'd be gone, and where would that leave her? Alone. So no matter how much she thought about him or second-guessed her commitment to moving forward with Keith, being with Ransom was a far less viable option.

With her throat uncomfortably tight, she finished washing the dishes then went to find Ransom in the living room, where he was standing over the computer. Sheets of paper whispered out of the printer at the end of the desk.

"I'm going to leave now," she announced.

He looked up in surprise. "Why?"

"It's getting late."

It would be dark soon, and she definitely shouldn't be here then. She'd already dry-humped him in bed. Sick or not, he presented a temptation she found hard to resist.

He nodded, a rueful twist to his mouth. "Thanks for coming," he said.

"You're welcome." She picked up her purse and hugged it to her chest. "Bye." Why didn't she move? "Promise me you'll move forward on the restaurant idea."

His smile was slight, feigning lightheartedness, the same as she. "I promise."

One foot in front of the other, Sophie.

"Take care," she said, feeling weepy.

She rushed toward the door, her upper lip trembling as she fought an overpowering urge to cry. Leaving him tore at her heart.

Outside in the hallway, she pressed her thumb hard against the elevator button and stepped into the cabin when it arrived on the floor. Closing her eyes, she leaned against the interior wall.

Why was it so hard to stay away? She rubbed her chest, where a sharp ache had developed.

Why did it hurt so much to leave?

****

The apartment seemed extra empty with her gone. The absence of Sophie's caring and vibrant personality left Ransom feeling desolate and hollow.

He dropped into the chair and buried his head in his hands. He should go back to bed, but that was the last thing he wanted to do. Talking to Sophie gave him some ideas, and he needed to order supplies to carry them out. It would take thirty minutes, an hour at the most, to search online for what he needed. After all, he'd promised Sophie he'd move forward, and that was what he intended to do.

Ransom rolled his neck and clicked on his favorite website for dishes and cookware. He scrolled down the page, adding items to the cart as he went. He could feel his pulse accelerate as he found each new item. At the end of forty-five minutes, he had everything he thought he'd need, at least for now. And for the first time in years, he placed a substantial order, then sat back...and smiled.

Chapter Eighteen

Sophie entered the home of her longtime friends, Jay and Brenda Santorini, and they all exchanged hugs. Brenda was the editor of an entertainment magazine and Jay owned a marketing firm. They were her oldest and dearest friends, and had shocked everyone by getting married right after the holidays, after being in love for years and suffering in silence. She couldn't be happier for them as a couple, and for the baby on the way.

"Look at you." Sophie crouched in front of her friend and placed her hands on Brenda's two-month pregnant belly. "Hello in there," Sophie said, even though her friend wasn't showing yet.

Brenda laughed, ever chic looking in a maxi dress, her short hair smoothed low on her head, and her dark skin glowing.

"Stop it, crazy woman." Brenda looped arms with her, and they went into the dining room with Jay, where a spread of eggplant parmesan, salad, and crusty garlic bread awaited.

Sophie inhaled deeply, pulling the scent of homemade marinara sauce, garlic, and oregano into her nostrils. "Mmmm. I can't wait. I'm starving."

They sat around the table and dived into the delicious food, and soon the conversation turned to the problem at hand—the ongoing custody battle between Jay and his ex-wife, Jenna. Their twin sons were supposed to move in with Jay this fall, but Jenna was fighting against it.

"She won't budge, and I feel as if this nightmare won't end," Jay, a tall, dark Italian, said. Frustration echoed in his lightly accented voice—the way it always did whenever he discussed the situation with his ex-wife.

Brenda, seated across from Sophie, covered his hand with hers. "She won't give up," she explained to Sophie. "Her latest accusation is that we got married to make her look bad, to influence the judge to rule in our favor."

Hard to believe they all used to be friends—Jay, Brenda, Sophie, and Jenna—part of a group of six that had known each other since their twenties. When Jay and Brenda decided to pursue a relationship, their decision turned an already volatile situation volcanic.

Jay and Jenna's court battle was a sordid one that, if Sophie hadn't witnessed it herself, she might not have believed to be true. Jay and Jenna had been married for a short time years ago, and had two sons, fraternal twins Arturo and Marco. Later, they learned that Arturo was Jay's son and Marco was the son of a man named Dale Armstrong, and they found out purely by chance. With Jenna carrying the color-blind gene and Dale also being color-blind, the chances of having a son that was color-blind increased dramatically from twenty-five percent to fifty percent, resulting in Marco having the same issue as his biological father.

"I still can't believe how she purposely misled you all those years. She made this mess," Sophie said. She'd lost all respect for her former friend, and crossed her fingers in the hope that Jay won the right to have his biological son, and the son he'd helped raise all those years, with him in Atlanta.

"Our attorney doesn't think there will be an end anytime soon. We're definitely going to have to go to court," Jay said. "We thought this would be a short and quick process, but the past six months have been nothing but constant fighting, with the boys caught in the middle."

Dale wanted his son in Florida and wanted to spend time getting to know him. Jay, on the other hand, had already planned to take full custody of the boys, starting this fall. The fact that Marco was not his biological son did not stop him from wanting to take both boys. He had been his father for eleven years—raised him, loved him, taken care of him—and he couldn't imagine splitting the boys up.

Jenna didn't want the boys split up either, and had rescinded her offer to have them live with Jay in Atlanta. If Marco could not go, neither could Arturo, as far as she was concerned. And that was why they were headed to court.

"Is there anything I can do to help?" Sophie asked.

Her friends looked at each other.

"We might need you to testify about what you've observed, regarding my relationship with the boys,"

Jay said.

"Gladly," Sophie said firmly. "Just tell me when."

Jay let out a relieved breath. "I knew I could count on you. I just wish it didn't have to come to this. We could avoid a trial altogether if Jenna would stop fighting me on custody."

"But she won't. Because she's angry at me and you for getting together," Brenda said.

Which was all true. Jenna disliked the couple immensely, and clearly was not above using her sons to hurt them.

They finished dinner, and Jay went into the home office to work while Sophie and Brenda sat in the living room chatting. Sophie pulled her feet under her bottom and rested an arm on the sofa. Beside her, Brenda elevated her feet on an ottoman.

"I hope this mess with the boys gets wrapped up soon," Brenda said with a sigh.

"It will. You just have to be confident. How did the trip to Naples go?" A few weeks ago, Jay and Brenda made a trip to Jay's home country to meet his mother, since she had been unable to make it to the States for the wedding.

"Better than expected," her friend admitted with a wide grin. "You know how Jay's father is." The older Santorini male was a difficult man who constantly complained about how Jay ran the family business, and had strongly suggested Jay's second wife should be an Italian woman. "But his mother is so sweet. She is an absolute doll and gave me a few recipes that I could use to make dishes for him and our future *bambinos*." She rested a hand on her flat stomach.

One day, Sophie thought, looking at her friend with a bit of envy. Despite the drama surrounding their family now, she knew Brenda was happy. She'd married the man she loved and was expecting her first child.

"Oh gosh, I've been talking about myself all night. What about you? What's the latest?"

Brenda didn't approve of her relationship with Keith, having firsthand knowledge of the breakups and makeups over the years. Both she and Jay thought when she and Keith broke up the last time, that would be the end of their relationship for good. Now Sophie was too embarrassed to mention Keith had cheated on her. It would only confirm what they thought of him, and confirm that she should have left him in the past.

"Nothing to tell. Keith and I are good."

"Oh?" Brenda raised a brow, skepticism easy to discern in her voice.

"He's changed a lot recently."

Brenda pursed her lips. "You know you're my best friend."

"Yesss."

Brenda put up her hands. "I'm not going to lecture you. I just...hope that you guys can get it together this time. This back and forth thing you're always doing doesn't make for an emotionally healthy relationship. You should be with someone who makes you feel good. All the time."

Someone like Ransom.

"He makes me feel good. I'm his priority now."

"I hope so, Sophie." Brenda took her hand and squeezed. "Because that's what you deserve. Don't waste your time with a man who doesn't appreciate you."

"I won't. I've learned my lesson from the past. I

won't ever stay with a man who doesn't appreciate me again."

Chapter Nineteen

Ransom pulled his car into the driveway of his brother's two-story neocolonial house on a quiet street in an Atlanta suburb. He was halfway up the walkway when the front door was yanked open from the inside. His brother's wife, Shawna, stood on the threshold, her smiling brown face fuller than when he saw her at Christmas, in Oklahoma at his parents' house.

"Hey, stranger," she said. "Glad you decided to take a break and grace us with your presence."

Ransom gave Shawna a hug, and her pregnant belly pressed into him, an indication of the upcoming addition to their four-member family.

"Hey yourself, fatty."

She slapped his chest, and he feigned hurt, groaning and stumbling backward.

Shawna laughed at his theatrics. "Come on in. Ryan and the kids are out back."

The mouth-watering scent of dinner perfumed the house as he followed her swinging ponytail into the kitchen.

"What are you making?"

"I have a pot roast in the slow cooker getting extra tender and delicious. Mashed potatoes will be finished soon, and there's green beans and roasted corn brushed with the honey your aunt sent from her bee farm."

Ransom rubbed his hands together. "Sounds good. Can't wait."

"Can I get you something to drink?" Shawna asked, as she puttered around the kitchen.

"I'll get it. What do you have?"

Standing at the sink, she looked over her shoulder at him. "Um…there's beer in the fridge, water, and a few minutes ago I made a fresh pitcher of iced tea, so it's not cold yet."

"I'll take a beer." He walked over to the refrigerator.

"Would you grab one for Ryan, too?"

"Sure thing."

He pulled out two bottles of Full Moon pale ale, opened them, and exited through the French doors into the privacy-fenced back yard. Ryan sat on a plastic lawn chair watching Madison chase Ryker around the swing set with her lips puckered and making kissing noises. She was a very affectionate little girl, and always trying to kiss someone.

Ransom grinned as he watched them play. Madison had a head full of curly hair pulled to the top of her head. At almost three years old, she did well to keep up with her brother, who was ten months older.

"You made it. Pull up a chair." Ryan pointed to

the chairs stacked against the back wall of the house.

Ransom handed his brother one of the beers, and sat down beside him.

"Of course. You and Shawna make it sound as if I wouldn't come."

Ryan shrugged. "We know how it's been in the past. I figured something might come up at work and you'd have to cancel."

Ransom winced. True, he'd cancelled trips to Atlanta in the past, and since his temporary move to Atlanta over a month ago, this was the first time he'd ventured outside Midtown to the suburbs to see his family. He really needed to do better.

"I took this afternoon off."

"Good for you." Ryan knocked his bottle against Ransom's.

They both had dark hair and blue eyes, but that was where the similarities ended. Ryan was a few years younger and, to Ransom's way of thinking, very impulsive. He'd done the unthinkable and dropped out of college to pursue a career in furniture making. Not exactly a growth industry, but he'd turned it into a profitable business after following his heart instead of listening to the naysayers.

The story of how he met his wife—while involved with another woman—was the height of impulsiveness. At the time, Ransom had expressed doubts about their relationship lasting, and true enough it hadn't, at first.

Fast-forward years later, and they'd been married almost six years and still behaved like newlyweds. They were the kind of couple that made other people roll their eyes. In fact, at his parents' house in Oklahoma, he caught them slow dancing in the living room late one night. He watched as his brother twirled his wife in a circle and then pulled her close, their bodies swaying as one in time to the R&B tunes coming through the speakers.

Ryan had seen him and said, "This is how I won her over. With my dance moves. Still got it."

They were one of the few married couples he could point to and say were genuinely happy. With each other and with their life.

"Hey, not so rough," Ryan scolded when Ryker shoved his sister to the ground. "Both of you come over here and say hi to Uncle Ransom."

Ryker helped his sister up and the two of them raced over.

"Uncle Wansom!" Madison said excitedly. He leaned down and she clutched his face, planting a wet kiss to his cheek.

"My baby brother is inside Mommy's tummy," Ryker announced.

"Is that right?" Ransom said.

"Uh-huh. She let us touch him. He was moving." He sounded in awe.

Beside him, Madison's eyes were wide in her face, and she bobbed her head up and down. "Inside Mommy."

"Uncle Ransom, you want to hand-wrestle?" Ryker asked hopefully.

"Aw man, you beat me so bad the last time."

The little boy giggled. "You need to practice."

"Yeah, I know. All right, let's do this."

He set his elbow on his knee and he and Ryker locked hands.

"Go!" Ryan said.

At first Ransom didn't budge his hand, and his

nephew's face contorted as he fought to push it down. Ransom groaned, pretending to struggle under the little boy's strength.

His sister jumped up and down beside him and chanted her encouragement. "Go, Wyker! Go! Go!"

Ransom allowed Ryker to slowly push his hand all the way down. He groaned in defeat, and Madison and Ryker jumped around excitedly.

"I won again!" Ryker said.

Ransom waved his hand back and forth as if it hurt. "Man, you're getting stronger."

"Me, me." Madison came forward with big, pleading eyes. "I want...I want."

"You want to beat me, too?" Ransom asked.

She nodded vigorously. Beside him, Ryan chuckled at her enthusiasm.

Ransom went through the same process, but allowing Madison to use both of her hands. Like before, he watched her fix her face into a concentrated scowl and then he let her slowly drag his arm down. He let out a puff of defeated air, and Madison squealed in her victory, jumping up and down again.

"You cheated. You have to use one hand," Ryker said.

"But...but I'm small." Madison stuck out her lower lip and looked at her father for reassurance.

"You did fine," Ryan said. "Good job. Both of you." He tweaked the nose of his little princess. Crisis over, she skipped away and Ryker followed. Soon, they were chasing each other around the yard again.

"When did you say Shawna was due?"

"In a couple of months. August."

"You have a name picked out?" Ransom plucked a

blade of grass.

"We've tossed around a few that begin with the letter R, but nothing definite yet. Hell, we may make up a name."

Ransom rotated the bottle in his hand. "How's business?" he asked.

"Business at Shawna's boutique is steady. She hired someone else the other day—to start training them for when the baby comes and she has to take leave. Did I tell you I'm planning to move the shop? I found a better location in Cabbagetown, which will cut my commute time. What's going at the law firm?"

"Same old, same old."

From the corner of his eye, he saw Ryan turn toward him. "That's an odd answer. Something wrong?"

"Everything's fine. I'm pretty sure I'll make partner soon."

"Congratulations. That's what you want, right?"

Ransom took a moment to answer, rubbing the condensation from the bottle with a thumb. "Sometimes I wonder if I should be doing something else."

"Like what?"

"I've thought about opening a restaurant, actually." Tension radiated from his stomach at the admission. He couldn't believe he'd spoken his dream aloud.

"*Opening a restaurant?*" The incredulity in Ryan's voice almost made him smile. "I knew you liked to cook, but I had no idea you had an interest in taking it that far. Restaurants have a high failure rate, don't they? Something like ninety percent in the first year?"

"That's an exaggeration. The numbers aren't that

high." Based on research, he'd seen significantly lower numbers, closer to sixty percent, and some sources quoted figures much lower.

"Since when did you get an interest in the restaurant business?"

"Ever since I worked at that restaurant with Mr. Lang's brother back in high school."

"Huh. I thought you hated that job."

"I did at first, because it kept me from doing all the fun stuff I wanted to with my friends, but at some point I started looking forward to going in." He'd even picked up extra shifts whenever he could. From washing dishes to waiting tables to cooking on the line, he'd learned a lot in those two years. He no longer felt adrift in a boat without a paddle or motor or even a compass to guide his way. The routine and no-nonsense attitude of the owner gave him the structure he needed.

Ryan took a swig of beer, his eyes trained on the kids as Ryker pushed Madison in one of the swings.

"Higher, Wyker! Higher!" she yelled.

"There's no law against changing careers," Ryan said. "People do it all the time."

Ransom let out a little laugh. Sophie had said something similar. "So I'm told."

"So are you telling me you plan to quit practicing law to open a restaurant?" His brother still sounded confused about the direction of the conversation.

"No." Ransom lifted the beer to his lips and swallowed.

Walking away from Abraham, MacKenzie & Wong was an unfathomable decision when he was so close to achieving his goal. He couldn't live like Shawna and Ryan—at least, he didn't think he could.

They weren't poor, but they certainly weren't rich either, and although they didn't seem to want for anything, he doubted he'd be satisfied living as simply as they did.

A partnership meant more than just money to support his lifestyle of expensive clothes, luxury cars, and fine dining. It offered the prestige of saying he'd arrived, and effectively showed his doubters that he was successful and better than just "shit."

"What kind of food would you serve if you did open a restaurant?" Ryan asked.

"Pure Americana, farm to table. Hearty burgers, fresh vegetables, and melt-in-your-mouth steaks. I might even incorporate a vegetarian menu." Thanks to Sophie, he'd considered incorporating more vegetarian options.

"Sounds like you've thought a lot about something you don't plan to do."

Ransom didn't deny or agree. "One of these days I'll cook and have you guys over for dinner."

The door behind them opened. "Dinner's almost ready. Come in and get cleaned up," Shawna called.

His niece and nephew raced ahead of them, and Ransom and Ryan followed more slowly. They helped Shawna place the food, plates, and utensils on the table.

Seated in the dining room, they all held hands and Ryan said grace. As Ransom watched his family—Ryan and Shawna with their heads bent and the kids fidgeting impatiently in their chairs—he envied their domesticity a little bit. He used to think thirty-seven was young, but in truth, he was nearing middle age, and he was nowhere near having any of this. No complaints about screaming kids climbing into bed early on Saturday morning to rob him of sleep. No wife to comfort him after a long day, or nag him when he needed to do better. He didn't have any of that. Not even close.

There was something missing, a thought that crossed his mind more and more lately—ever since a certain gray-eyed beauty came into his life.

Chapter Twenty

A tasting party was a brilliant idea, and Sophie couldn't wait to see what Ransom had in store. He promised a variety of small-plate dishes, including a substantial selection of vegetarian options, but didn't elaborate or offer a hint of what was on the menu.

She arrived at his door with a combination of excitement and trepidation in her stomach. She finally settled on pale-colored slacks and a green shirt, but she'd lost track of how many times she changed clothes, and couldn't admit even to herself that the real reason she'd struggled with what to wear was because she wanted to impress Ransom and his brother and sister-in-law, who were also attending the dinner. He'd told her she could bring a couple of friends, and she invited Brenda and Jay, two foodies she knew would give their honest opinion but would also enjoy a night out with a great meal.

A young woman opened Ransom's front door.

Her appearance so surprised Sophie, she forgot to be polite and just stared, sizing up the other woman and unable to find fault. She was pretty, blonde, and wore a generous smile on her friendly face.

"Hello! I'm Sandy. You must be Sophie?"

Sophie snapped out of the shock and returned the smile. "Yes, I am."

"Nice to meet you. Ransom's in the kitchen putting the finishing touches on one of the dishes."

Sophie entered and was immediately blown away by the transformation. The large front room had been rearranged into an intimate setting. A table was covered with a pale-yellow tablecloth with seating for eight. Large clear vases strategically placed around the room held small votive candles. Sample-sized food lined the middle of the table and the large cherry wood buffet against the wall, with the name of the dishes printed on a small rectangular card that sat in front of each platter. Piano music played softly in the background.

Sophie was amazed at the spread, which was a feast not only for the eyes, but for the nose. "Wow. This looks amazing."

"Thanks. We've been hard at work all day."

We?

Sophie eyed the woman, wondering where she'd come from and why he'd invited her. Now she, Sophie, would be the odd man out because she was the only one in attendance that wasn't part of a couple.

In the kitchen, she found Ransom chopping parsley. In his big hand, the knife moved swiftly along the cutting board. She felt a stirring in her belly as she watched him.

"You cooked for an army," Sophie said.

He sprinkled the chopped herb onto individual cubes of lasagna, lined up on a long, narrow serving dish. "I had to increase the number of dishes because *somebody* doesn't eat meat."

He was wearing a black stud in his ear tonight, and for some reason the addition of the jewelry stepped up his sexy quotient. She'd always been indifferent about men wearing jewelry, particularly earrings, but it worked for Ransom. The air of edginess definitely permeated his appearance, especially when coupled with the slate-gray long-sleeved shirt and dark pants, both of which seemed to make him appear taller and broader than usual.

"How long did it take you to prepare all of this?" Sophie asked.

"All day. I'm exhausted."

"But you're smiling."

"I feel...alive." He frowned. "And maybe even a little nervous." He laughed.

"Well, the others better get here soon, or we'll have to start without them."

"Ransom, since you're all done, I'm going to head out."

Sophie had forgotten Sandy was standing behind her, and she felt almost guilty at ignoring the other woman's presence.

"You're leaving?" Sophie asked, surprised but unable to stop the jump of excitement her heart made.

"Yes, I'm afraid so. I hope you all enjoy everything."

"Give me just one second," Ransom said to Sophie, before following Sandy out of the kitchen.

She shouldn't, but Sophie peered around the corner at them as they said their goodbyes. She saw Ransom hand the young woman an envelope and breathed a sigh of relief. She had been hired to help and wasn't his girlfriend. Catching herself, Sophie shook her head in disgust. She shouldn't care.

"Everything's set," Ransom said. He rubbed his hands together and assessed the room.

"Can I help you with anything?" Sophie asked.

"No, I think that's it until the first guest—"

The sound of the doorbell interrupted him.

"The first guests," he said.

It was Brenda and Jay, and Sophie introduced the three to each other, and Ransom's brother and sister-in-law arrived a few minutes later. All four of them widened their eyes at the selections.

"Two pregnant women in the house. More wine for us," Sophie said.

They laughed and settled down on each long side of the table, ready for the parade of flavors that were about to hit their tongues. Brenda sat between Jay and Sophie. Ransom settled in across from Sophie, and his brother sat between him and his wife.

The choices included delicate cuts of steak, and even while they ate, Ransom continued to bring out dishes. Sophie helped when she could, clearing the table and setting a new dish before the group, like the parmesan-crusted steak fries, which were a big hit. The vegetarian options were all popular, too, particularly the portobello mushroom burger, which Ransom had sliced into miniature pieces, and Sophie complained there wasn't enough of.

The four-cheese spinach lasagna received thumbs up all around, including from Jay, who professed,

"I'm Italian, and I can tell you, this is some damn good lasagna."

The beef stew did not fare so well. The meat eaters all unanimously declared the dish the dud of the evening, but every other morsel was devoured with relish and washed down with wine or water between conversations that ranged from Shawna offering Brenda baby advice, to Ryan pointing out that his brother needed to move to Atlanta so they could have these parties more often.

"If Ransom moved here, that would make Sophie happy, I'm sure," Shawna said. She smiled knowingly across the table.

"Excuse me?" Sophie said.

"I'm sure you'd love if Ransom moved here permanently." The table went quiet, and Shawna looked around. "I'm sorry, did I say something wrong?"

Ransom cleared his throat and set down his wine glass. "Sophie and I are just friends. She has a man in her life already."

"Oh. I thought... You know what, I'm going to keep my mouth shut," Shawna said.

"And just think, she didn't even have any wine tonight," Ryan teased.

Shawna hid her face in her husband's shoulder, while the others had a good laugh at her expense.

But Ransom wasn't laughing. He was looking across the table at Sophie, and she was looking across the table at him.

"I made an honest mistake," Shawna said, her tone apologetic as she looked from Ransom to Sophie.

All eyes turned to Sophie, and she had the distinct impression they expected some kind of explanation.

Why, if she had a man, wasn't he here at the party, and she was instead looking as if she was paired up with Ransom?

"He couldn't make it," Sophie said, swallowing hard. Because she'd never asked him, and until that moment, hadn't given him any thought.

Ransom drained his glass. "More wine?" he said to no one in particular, holding the bottle aloft.

"I'll have a little more," Jay said. He extended his glass.

Fortunately, the conversation turned again to more mundane topics and the mood lightened, but Shawna's comment caused Sophie to think about what-ifs. What if she and Ransom were a couple? Then the gathering tonight could be the beginning of a tradition of more tasting parties and friendly conversations over wine and good food.

The little twinge in her chest, right below her left breast, which appeared whenever Ransom was near, sharpened that much more.

During a lull in the conversation, Ryan consulted his watch. "It's probably time for us to get out of here. I need to put this one to bed." He patted his wife's thigh.

Shawna was leaning against him, one arm wrapped around his arm and her head on his shoulder. She wore a pleasant smile on her face, but a heaviness in her eyes. "I can't seem to last as long as I used to. With this pregnancy I get worn out so fast. This boy drains all my energy." She gently rubbed her belly and straightened in the chair.

"Nobody leaves without taking some of this food." Ransom pointed in the general direction of the leftovers on the serving platters. Although they'd eaten a lot over the past few hours, there was still plenty left over.

"All right, all right, you've twisted my arm," his brother said. He and Shawna stood.

"I'm calling dibs on the cauliflower gratin. That's all mine," Sophie said, standing as well.

"Oh, come on," Brenda said, and a good-natured argument ensued, during which Sophie offered her a tablespoonful to take, and Ryan said he was calling dibs because of the familial relationship.

Jay took out a business card and handed it to Ransom. "When people are arguing over leftovers, that's when you know you're a helluva good cook. If you ever want to move into the restaurant business, call me. We can help you with the marketing." Jay's firm was the largest in the southeast.

"Start with catering," Brenda suggested, her eyes lighting up at the idea. She picked up a couple of platters to take into the kitchen. "My mother's getting married in a few months. Think you can come up with a menu for an evening wedding?"

"The man's a lawyer, not a caterer. Leave him alone and let's get some of these leftovers before Shawna and Ryan clean them out." Jay nudged her along.

"We can hear you," Shawna called from the kitchen.

While the four of them continued their argument in the kitchen, Ransom stared down at the business card. He seemed lost in thought before he finally realized Sophie was observing him. He cocked a brow.

I told you, she mouthed.

He smiled and the dimples made an appearance,

softening his features. He appeared happy, but subdued, and tucked the card into a pocket.

They took the rest of the dishes into the kitchen, and Sophie helped by scraping scraps into the trash and loading the dishwasher. Anything that couldn't fit was stacked in the sink and on the counters.

Brenda, Jay, Shawna, and Ryan said their goodbyes with their containers and wrapped plates, but Sophie remained behind. She wanted to find out Ransom's thoughts on the evening.

When he closed the door, he turned to face her. The room was quiet except for the music that continued to play in the background. Several of the candles had burned out, but a few remained to cast an ambient glow on the room.

"You were amazing tonight. I'm so happy for you," Sophie said.

"I wouldn't have done it without your encouragement."

Ransom let out a triumphant growl and lifted her off the floor. Sophie squealed, surprised but delighted. She hadn't been sure if he was happy or not, but evidently he'd been holding in his excitement. She laughed and flung her arms around his neck, just as excited as he was, as he spun them in a full circle in the middle of the room.

"They couldn't get enough," he said, his blue eyes shining like bright stars.

"I know. You were a hit."

"Except for beef stew."

"It was the only thing that was off."

"But they liked everything else."

"They *loved* everything else. The food was delicious. Restaurant quality for sure."

"The only thing I didn't make was the apple pie."

"You can't do everything. And frankly, I'm going to that bakery tomorrow to get one for myself."

She giggled, and he laughed again, a hearty, soul-lifting sound, and spun her around.

In the middle of the spin, his face changed, the expression of laughter easing away.

"There's still pie left, if you want it." His breathing became slightly irregular.

"I do." The fingertips of one hand traced the wavy hair at the back of his neck. She had no right to touch him like this, but she couldn't seem to help herself. "I want it."

The hands on the back of her thighs tightened a fraction and heat tugged at the apex of legs. She inhaled sharply and almost closed her eyes against the sensation. There was no other feeling in the world like being touched by him.

Right now she wanted him to kiss her. The anticipation was so keen, she edged her mouth closer. The instrumental music in the background acted like a soundtrack and increased to a crescendo. Aching tension built between them.

"Wrap your legs around me," Ransom said, his voice sounding raw.

Her legs cinched around his waist, and with one hand at her bottom and the other at her neck, he moved backward and sat on the arm of the sofa.

Sophie settled onto the hard thrust in his pants, and they both groaned as their lips seared together. One hand lifted into her loose hair and cupped her nape. While her mouth moved over his, his thumb stroked the sensitive skin behind her ear. His moist tongue slipped between her lips and did a searching sweep of her mouth. He reexamined the interior, angling his head to take the kiss even deeper.

She sighed into his mouth and held on tight. His kisses were like heaven. She tasted the fruity wine and the sweet apple dessert. She tasted *him*, and the extent of her hunger forced her to shift her body so that she could center the ridge of his hard erection along the cleft between her legs.

She'd fought this feeling for so long. This painful, demanding ache for him. Only Ransom made her feel like this—so out of control, so desperate for his possession she wanted to scream with frustration and beg him to take her all at the same time.

She undid the buttons on his shirt and lowered her lips to the exposed skin.

"I want to lick you here," he said, pressing his thumb between her legs and hitting right on her clit. Just like a bull's-eye.

She whimpered and licked his neck in retaliation. She kissed his ear and licked the lobe and earring. "I want to do the same to you," she breathed, cupping the bulge in his pants.

He grunted and bit her bottom lip.

"And lick you here," he said, dragging his thumb over her nipple.

"Yes. Please lick me there."

Without another word, he lifted up and turned her onto her back on the sofa.

Chapter Twenty-one

Maybe he'd wake up and this would all be a dream, but right now Ransom couldn't believe Sophie lay beneath him.

Impatiently, he pushed up her shirt and sucked an erect nipple through the black lace. He dragged his teeth over the little button and she gasped, wiggling her curvy body against him.

He pulled the shirt over her head, hungry for more of her exposed skin, while she released the back clasp of her bra, freeing her breasts into his waiting hands.

"You have the most perfect breasts." Ransom pressed the soft mounds together and dropped a kiss to her scented cleavage.

Everything about her turned him on. He adored her body, the amber skin versus the coppery tint of the tips of her breasts, the softness, the curves. With the palm of his hand, Ransom traced a line down the length of her torso, and she lifted into his touch. He showered kisses onto her skin, along the underside of her breasts and down to her stomach, drawing a moist circle around her navel with his tongue.

He groaned in frustration when he had to unbutton her pants. "Why'd you wear pants tonight? To torture me?"

She let out a breathless little laugh, and he went back to her mouth, moving his lips over hers in a deep, drugging kiss.

If she'd worn a skirt or a dress, he could tear off her panties and be inside her within minutes. Because that's where he was desperate to be right now.

He burrowed a hand down her open pants, gliding over the soft curls to the warm, slippery spot between her legs. The breathless little mew she let out was a reward in itself. He imagined the moment when he'd slide between her legs and be enveloped right *there*.

Biting his bottom lip, he inserted his middle finger inside her and flattened the heel of his hand against her clit. Her mouth fell open and her eyes fluttered closed. Thrusting the digit in and out, Ransom rubbed his hand over her mound. She grabbed him by the head and purred, a sexy sound that sent shivers racing up and down his spine. Her fingers dug into his scalp, and her hips lifted into each thrust of his finger.

"Ransom." That begging tone in her voice sent his mouth back to her neck. She arched her throat to his kisses while his hand continued to work inside her pants.

"Tell me what you want," he said. "Whatever you want, I'll—"

The jarring, bell-like sound threw him off his rhythm. That couldn't be the doorbell. It had to be his imagination.

The sound came again, and Sophie's undulating hips went still. Her gray eyes, darkened with passion, widened as they stared into his.

No, no, no. Who the hell was that? If he didn't answer, maybe they'd go away.

Instead of going away, the person pounded on the door.

Sophie swallowed, and Ransom practically saw the desire drain from her face.

"Ransom, it's me, Ryan," his brother called on the other side of the door.

Ransom swore, dropped his head to Sophie's shoulder, and reluctantly eased his hand from between her legs.

"You should answer the door." She pushed his chest and forced him off her. While he rolled to his feet, she grabbed her shirt and tugged it over her head.

"Don't move," he said, but she ignored him and scampered off in the direction of the bathroom.

The doorbell rang again.

"I'm coming!" Ransom roared. He repositioned his hard penis and pulled the shirt over his pants to hide the bulge.

When he opened the door, Ryan frowned at him. "What took you so long?"

"What do you want?" Ransom asked.

His brother surveyed his rumpled appearance, and Ransom could only imagine what he looked like in the creased shirt with his hair a mess from Sophie running her fingers through it.

"Er, did I interrupt something?" Ryan raised an eyebrow.

Ignoring the question, Ransom peered past him to

the hallway. "Where's Shawna?"

"She's in the car. In our rush to get out of here with all that food, she forgot her purse. She said it should be on the floor next to the chair she sat in."

Sure enough, Ryan found the black purse tucked under the table next to the chair leg. "Got it." He held it up for Ransom to see and walked back to the door. "Dinner was great, by the way. Maybe the restaurant thing isn't such a bad idea."

"I'll think about it." Ransom rubbed the back of his neck. He was completely distracted and wanted Ryan out of there so he could get back to Sophie.

"Do that." His brother stepped toward the door, but as he walked through, he cast a final glance inside the apartment. "By the way, tell Sophie I said good night." He ambled away with a smile on his face.

Ransom shut the door and right away spotted Sophie's bra half hidden under one of the pillows. He groaned inwardly. Ryan must have seen it, too.

"He's gone."

A few seconds later, Sophie walked out, clothes rearranged and hair smoothed down, but under the shirt, her nipples stood out like little marbles. Ransom's penis jumped. He wanted those nipples back in his mouth, the urge so strong he forced his eyes from the tempting way they pushed against the material.

She swallowed.

"Talk to me," he said quietly, a swell of unease taking over the insides of his stomach.

"We shouldn't have done that."

"I disagree."

"Keith—"

"I don't care about Keith," Ransom growled.

"Well, I do. He's my boyfriend. You and me...I don't know what we are or what we're doing." Sophie pressed a palm to her forehead. "I'm afraid."

"Of me?"

"No." Sophie dropped her hands and looked around the room, as if searching for the answers. Her pained expression hurt, twisted like a knife in his chest. He hated to be the cause of her pain, the reason for her unhappiness. "Of me. Of this." She pointed between them.

He waited for her to elaborate.

"I don't know what to do," she said.

"You know what to do." He went to her and cupped her slender jaw in his hands.

She stepped away from him, away from his touch. His arms fell to his sides but longed to touch her again.

"In the Bahamas, you said you didn't want a relationship," Sophie said.

"I never—"

"Yes, you did. You said relationships were too distracting and too demanding of your time."

So much had happened since then that it seemed like the conversation took place ages ago, but she was right. He'd developed a motto after the breakup with Lisa. No commitments. No girlfriends. But spending time with Sophie had made him reconsider. He no longer thought his life revolved around a square room morning, noon, and night, and there was more to life than hearings and legal briefs.

"I don't feel that way anymore," Ransom assured her.

"Since when?"

"Since you. You don't have to be afraid. I won't

177

hurt you."

"I don't know that, and I'm terrified that what we think we feel isn't real. That it's hormones or just chemistry, a sexual attraction that will eventually pass." She sighed. "The truth is, you're almost exactly like Keith."

"I'm nothing like him," Ransom said, a hard note to his voice.

Slowly, Sophie shook her head. "I'm not so sure. At least the way he used to be—driven, hardworking, and there's nothing wrong with that. Those are wonderful qualities, but not when they're taken to the extreme."

"You expect me to just let you go?"

"I was never yours," Sophie said quietly. She stared down at her hands as the sound of the music continued to filter though the speakers. "I made him a promise." She lifted her gaze to his. "I promised I would give one hundred percent into repairing our relationship. He asked me for another chance, and I gave it. I intend to keep my word."

"Sophie—"

"You're making it hard to keep my promise. I'm going to stay away from you, and I need you to stay away from me."

"No way."

"Please."

"No."

"No more bike rides on Saturday. No more phone calls."

"Don't do this."

"I mean it. Just forget about me."

"How am I supposed to do that?"

She bit her lip. "Goodbye, Ransom."

She headed toward the door, but he grabbed her wrist. "You're making a mistake."

"It's my mistake to make." Sophie tugged her hand away and walked quickly out the door, leaving him behind in the empty apartment. Alone.

Ransom shuffled across the room and dropped onto the sofa. Lifting the bra from beneath the pillow, he crushed it to his face, and the scent of jasmine filled his nostrils.

How in the world was he supposed to forget her?

Chapter Twenty-two

The Atlanta residence of Brit and Suzette Wong was located in an exclusive part of town that boasted homes starting at one million dollars. Every year, the partners of Abraham, MacKenzie & Wong invited their top picks from the four offices around the country, creating an opportunity for the chosen ones to mingle and confirm they were deserving of the partnership before the final vote took place.

The food served always followed a theme, and this year's culinary choice paid homage to Brit's Chinese roots. Among the options were spring rolls and cubes of honey-glazed BBQ spare ribs on beds of green papaya, circulated by wait staff moving unobtrusively among the guests.

Ransom was enjoying a walnut-crusted prawn, talking with a fellow attorney from the New York office, when Sophie and Keith arrive. He'd been watching for them all night, but barely took notice of

Keith. After not seeing her for two weeks, Sophie had his undivided attention and took his breath away.

Her hair had been smoothed straight and pulled back into a tight ball. The dress she wore was exquisite, a simple black and white number, with a thigh-high split. It brushed the floor and fastened on the right shoulder. Bold red lipstick made her lips appear as soft and inviting as he knew they were. Large earrings dangled from her ears, but it was her eyes that caused a stampede in his chest. The gray popped and appeared particularly sultry beneath heavy, smoky makeup.

Ransom focused on maintaining rigid control, despite his hammering heart and watching Sophie and Keith with a mixture of jealousy and self-loathing. A faint tug in his belly appeared as they approached, deepening into a full-blown clawing sensation when she came to stand before him in a cloud of familiar floral perfume.

Introductions were made, and Sophie shook the hand of the other attorney present.

"Where's your date?" Keith asked, his hand resting on the curve of Sophie's hip. The question was directed at Ransom.

"I came alone," he responded.

"Huh," Keith said, as if pondering the answer. He nodded at the other attorney. "If you two will excuse us, there are some other people I'd like Sophie to meet."

With his hand at the small of her back, he led her away to a small group near the fireplace that included his parents, and Ransom realized Sophie hadn't said a word during the brief interlude.

"Lucky son of a bitch," the other attorney said.

"He's filthy rich and he gets to go home with her tonight."

The skin on the back of Ransom's neck crawled, and he watched Keith's hand rub up and down Sophie's back. A flash of memory came to him, of dragging his own hands up and down her spine, pulling her naked body on top of him to thrust up into her, and listening to her purr with pleasure as they made love.

He stalked over to a uniformed attendant. "I'll take one of those."

He swiped a glass of dark liquor from the tray and tossed back the liquid, letting the burn course down his throat. Brandy. Just what he needed to shake him out of this funk and give him clarity of thought.

These feelings for Sophie—this craving he had for her—would eventually pass. It had to. Maybe when he returned to Chicago.

He drained the rest of the liquid and finally dragged his gaze away from the object of his obsession.

Focus.

He was here to win over the partners. That's what he would concentrate on doing for the rest of the evening. He absolutely would not think about how Sophie would be spending the night with Keith. Or that she should be spending the night with him, instead.

****

Sophie laughed politely at the joke Brit Wong made. Keith's parents were funny and friendly, and so far she'd felt welcomed at their party. When she'd met them in Chicago and they learned of her three-year relationship with Keith, they appeared surprised that they hadn't met her before, but almost immediately covered that surprise with smiles and excuses about busy schedules and traveling.

The fact that Keith's parents knew nothing about her had confirmed that their relationship had never been a priority for him before, a sobering thought that made her review the off-and-on nature of their relationship over the years, the cancelled plans, and ultimately Keith's affair with the waitress.

Her thoughts strayed from the conversation at hand in a search for Ransom's location. She scanned the room, hoping not to be too obvious, and located him on a sofa near the fireplace, talking with one of the men Keith had pointed out as a managing partner.

"What is it that you do, Sophie?"

Hearing her name dragged her back into the discussion. Suzette Wong, wearing a red designer dress with a bandeau top and a small fortune in diamonds around her neck, waited with an expectant smile on her face, but she hadn't asked the question. A female attorney who'd joined the small circle, introduced earlier as Myriam and one of the youngest to be up for partner, according to Keith, had inquired after her profession.

"I'm a flight attendant," she answered.

"Fascinating. Crazy schedule, though, isn't it?" Myriam asked.

"Starting out, yes. The pay was mediocre and I didn't have a say in my schedule at all." Sophie laughed a little at the memory of the early days— barely making ends meet and looking forward to leftover airplane food just so she'd have a meal, sharing a crash pad with numerous other flight attendants to save money, and being on reserve, which made it impossible to make real plans because she could be called in with only two hours' notice. Those days were long gone, thank goodness. "In the airline industry, seniority is everything, and I'm nine years in now, which means better routes, flexibility in scheduling—which allows me up to ten days off a month if I plan right, yay!—and better pay."

"She has a degree in chemistry and a masters in marketing, but doesn't use either," Keith said.

"Oh, really?" Suzette said.

"I thought one day I'd like to take over my mother's juice shop and expand it into a chain of stores," Sophie explained, "but after less than a year, I learned real fast that managing a store wasn't what I wanted to do. I applied for the job at the airline on a whim because another friend of mine was applying. She didn't make it. I did."

"I told her before she needs to use that brain of hers," Keith said, squeezing her shoulder.

Sophie bristled under his touch. "I am using my brain," she said evenly.

"Not as much as you could."

"Are you suggesting that what I do doesn't require intelligence?"

"Come on, Sophie, you're a damn flight attendant. You're not doing brain surgery." Keith chuckled.

Sophie fought hard to maintain her composure because she didn't want to make a scene in front of the other three people, but she couldn't let the comments slide like she had in the past.

"I love my job. It's important to me. But I'm not *just* a flight attendant. I may not be doing brain surgery, but the safety of every passenger on the aircraft depends on me and the rest of the crew. That's a huge responsibility."

His face deflated. "Sophie, I didn't mean—"

"Maybe it's not prestigious enough for you, but it's a job that I love and allows me to travel and meet interesting and exciting people." She took a deep breath, tamping down the anger. "I have a couple of degrees, but let me clarify to you once and for all about my choices. Yes, there are a lot of jobs available to someone with my background. I could work in quality assurance, toxicology, or even for the government handling chemical health and safety. I could work for the military or for a lab or teach chemistry. My mother could hire me. Those are choices, Keith. Because having those degrees give me something to fall back on. Having those degrees offer me options. Having those degrees does *not* put a noose around my neck and force me into a box so that I have to do something that I don't want to."

Keith's face turned crimson. Myriam's lips formed a silent O and she averted her eyes across the room. Brit raised a brow, while the corners of Suzette's mouth hinted at a smile.

Sophie clasped her hands in front of her. "If you'll excuse me." She was heated and needed to calm down. She left them standing there and went out into the hall.

Chapter Twenty-three

Sophie found a spot where she could be alone down a corridor that led to a series of guest bedrooms and bathrooms. When she arrived earlier, she had placed an overnight bag in one of the bedrooms. Staying over didn't seem like a good idea anymore. She couldn't believe he'd belittled her work in front of other people.

She slipped out to the stone balcony and listened to the night—sounds of cars passing by on the highway, and closer, crickets chirping and the croak of a frog. She inhaled the air filled with the scent of gardenias from bushes lining the long driveway up to the house.

She knew the moment she was no longer alone. The scent of Ransom's expensive cologne replaced the fragrance of the flowers. The familiar scent was intoxicating and reminded her of his hands down her pants, wreaking havoc a mere two weeks ago.

"You shouldn't be out here with me," she said.

"I wanted to talk to you."

She ran her fingertips over the gravelly surface of the railing. "There's nothing to talk about, and it's inappropriate for us to be standing out here together. Someone might see us and misunderstand."

"Misunderstand what? We're two friends having a conversation."

Friends. She was starting to really hate that word.

She turned around to see him standing in the open doorway, hands stuffed into the pockets of his tuxedo pants. His eyes stared into hers, and a tingle of awareness ran down her bare arms.

"You're hiding," he said.

"I wouldn't say I'm hiding. I wanted to be alone."

"That should be my cue to walk away, but…" He strolled out and came to stand beside her, resting his forearms on the stone surface.

Sophie dragged her eyes away from his profile and looked out into the dark yard.

"Still working on your restaurant ideas?" she asked, to fill the quiet.

"Somewhat. What happened in there?" he asked.

"Nothing."

"Come on, tell me. You seemed upset."

Sophie hesitated, but after a short pause, she recounted the conversation with Keith and how his comment had belittled her work.

"He shouldn't have said that," Ransom said.

Guilt pricked her conscience. "And I shouldn't complain to you about him."

"Why not? We're friends."

"Friends who've been more than friendly."

"I didn't think you remembered."

"I want to forget." Heaven help her, even when she was with Keith, she thought about Ransom and longed for his touch.

"Why?" he asked quietly. Too quietly.

Maybe it was the cover of darkness that made her speak boldly, but Sophie heard herself say, "Because it's hard to be around you sometimes."

Yet she yearned to see him. She'd looked forward to tonight because she knew he'd be here.

"It's hard to be around you every time."

She swallowed. "I want my relationship with Keith to work."

"I don't believe that's true."

"It doesn't matter what you believe."

"Admit it," he prodded softly. "Admit that what happened between us was more than sex. In the Bahamas and the other night at my place. Admit that you feel what I do whenever I'm near you. It's more than attraction. It's a connection and we're wasting our time trying to fight it." He edged closer, and the hairs on her arms stood at attention. "You look amazing tonight." The back of his fingers trailed down her bare arm.

"Please don't." Sophie shivered, stepping away. "If someone sees us…"

"I don't care if anyone sees us."

"Well, I do." When he reached for her again, she knocked away his hand. "This isn't a game."

His jaw hardened into a rigid line. "I'm not playing a game. I've been telling myself that what I feel will eventually go away, but it hasn't. My feelings for you only get stronger. When I saw you on Saturdays, I was happy and frustrated at the same time because I knew I'd only get a few hours and then you'd be gone, and another week would pass before I'd see you again."

His words pricked her heart. "It wasn't easy for me, either. I was torn."

"You shouldn't be torn. You should know what you want. If you tell me you love him, I'll walk away and not bother you anymore."

Sophie briefly closed her eyes. "That's not fair."

He came closer and cornered her. "Tell me you love him. Say it."

Her heart thumped wildly. That should be an easy declaration to make.

His head bent toward hers, their lips almost brushing. "Tell. Me. You. Love. Him."

Sophie stood straighter instead of cowering in the corner. Looking him directly in the eyes, she said, "Leave me alone. It's too late. You don't care as much as you'd like to pretend. You're eventually going to leave here, just like you did in the Bahamas. You let me go. You didn't come after me." Her voice trembled, but she stared into his eyes, challenging him with her words.

Ransom stared at her, his chest heaving up and down as if he'd run a marathon. When he didn't respond, she shook her head in disgust and marched away. The dark corridor welcomed her back into the house, and she walked with purposeful steps away from him, resolving to steer clear of him moving forward.

Strong arms grabbed her from behind. "It's not too late," Ransom growled into her neck.

Her heart jumped and she gasped as he dragged her into a bedroom with a slice of light coming in through the window, and slammed the door.

Clutching her face in his big hands, Ransom stared

down at her, his eyes brilliant blue stones in the shadowy room. "Never, ever too late."

He fastened his mouth to hers, lips moving with a hard, sensual promise that dragged a moan from her throat and had her curling her fingers into the lapel of his jacket. He pressed her against the wall and wedged a muscular thigh between hers. One hand smoothed up her leg and gripped a butt cheek.

He ground his hips against hers, simulating sex, the erotic motion of his body sending her reeling into unbridled passion, reminding her of the immeasurable pleasure she experienced in his arms. The spot throbbing between her legs ached for him. His mouth traveled across her arched throat and he sucked on her chin, licking and nipping at her skin with his teeth.

There was only one way this could end, and Sophie wanted it. Wanted him. Desperately. They landed on the bed amid feverish kisses and groping hands, he on top of her as he caressed her hypersensitive breasts through the constricting bodice. He cupped the soft mounds and tweaked her nipples through the material, and a shiver racked her tightened body.

Sophie twisted beneath him as he showered kisses onto her bare neck and shoulder. When his hands reached under the dress, she lifted her hips to aid him in dragging her underwear past her knees, and he tossed it aside.

He kissed a path down her body through the clothes, the delicious pressure of his mouth searing as if he touched bare skin, spreading desire to the heated cleft between her thighs. Then he was forcing her legs apart. Strong hands kept them open so he could dive between her thighs, and Sophie let out a loud gasp at the contact, squirming against the intimate probe of his tongue.

She looked down at his dark head and bit her lip at the erotic sight of him fastened to the apex of her thighs. His lips moved with precision over her aching flesh. The wet smack of his lips and tongue sounded in the room as he devoured her. Wet and throbbing, she immediately broke apart. The climax left her trembling, panting, the sound of her harsh intake of breath adding to the crescendo of sexual noises emitted from his lips and throat.

Ransom offered her a brief reprieve, sliding his hands beneath her backside and gently kissing her inner and outer thighs. The added sensations were almost unbearable, and she twisted—a silent, desperate movement to escape him—but he dragged her back.

His lips fastened on her again. This time the gasp she released was louder, harsher—almost a plea for relief. She'd barely managed to catch her breath from the first orgasm. She still ached. Her body still tingled.

None of that mattered to Ransom.

The second time she came, the ripples rocked her harder, like waves pummeling a seashore. Her eyes rolled back. Her fingers clutched his hair as she cried out with a loud voice and only managed to stifle the sound at the end when she bit into her bottom lip. Exactly what he wanted. To make her scream. He wouldn't have been satisfied until she screamed.

Lifting off the bed, Ransom unzipped his pants. He tore open the condom wrapper and slipped on the rubber. Grabbing her behind the knees, he dragged her to the edge of the bed and entered with ease, the slippery entrance to her body offering not even a shred of resistance.

Sophie closed her limbs around him. What choice did she have but to hold on tight, fastening her legs around his hips and her arms around his back?

They rocked together, the squeak of the bed sounding loud in the quiet room as their bodies remembered and hearts connected.

Ransom cupped her face and gazed down at her. In the dark, her gray eyes were vivid and intense. Darker than he'd ever seen them before. Lying between her legs was a missed comfort—one that he never thought he'd experience again.

"This is me coming after you," he rasped.

His muscles bunched as he fought to endure and last a little longer. He moved his hips and she closed her eyes, lips separating as she savored the sensation of him inside her.

"This is me not letting you go." His voice was a low, guttural sound, thick with desire.

Her responsive body and desperate little sighs stripped away his control. He picked up speed and she matched his passion, thrusting upward, both of them straining toward repletion.

In the end, they shattered very close together. First Sophie, her body trembling beneath him and a hoarse cry flying from her throat. Ransom came next, a deep grunt signaling his release as the room rocked crazily around him. He blew a puff of air on her collarbone right before collapsing on top of her.

In the silence, their heavy breaths could be heard as they tried to regain control.

Ransom rolled onto his back and went into the adjoining bathroom to dispose of the condom. When he returned, Sophie sat on the edge of the bed, her shoulders bowed in a despondent curve. He sat down beside her.

"I'm not this person," she said.

"Sophie." He touched her back.

"It was supposed to be a one time thing. Not this need that won't go away." Her voice shook.

Ransom pulled her close, resting his face in the groove between her shoulder and chin. Inhaling her. Simply breathing her in.

"Tell me what you want," he said.

"Your time. Your attention. Everything."

"Then that's what I'll give you. Everything." He brushed the nape of her neck with his hand and saw the hesitation in her eyes. "We can't keep pretending there's nothing between us." It would be easier to remove his arm and pretend he still had two.

She eased from his arms and picked up her underwear. "I'm here with him, at his parents' house."

"Leave with me."

She shook her head. "I can't do that. Let me—"

"Why not?" Ransom stood and started fixing his clothes as well.

She was quiet as she tugged on her underwear.

"Why not, Sophie?" He grabbed her arms.

"Because you're here to ensure you receive the partnership."

"I don't care about that."

"Yes, you do. And I do, too. There's no way I'd let you leave a party that you'd regret walking out on the minute you go through the door. You want to be here. You need to be here. Tonight is a culmination of everything you've worked for over the past eleven years, and leaving together would be impulsive. I don't want you to lose this opportunity because of me."

Being impulsive was not his approach to decision-making, but his gut told him it might be necessary this time. He raked a hand through his hair. "I'm not leaving without you."

"You have to. I won't embarrass Keith in front of his colleagues and his family, and I know how important tonight is for you. I won't let you ruin your chances."

"Listen to me—"

"No, you listen." She pressed a soft hand against his chest. "Go. I'll meet you later."

"Where?"

"At your place."

"I don't like this." He raked his fingers through his hair. "I'm not leaving you alone with him."

"Let me handle Keith. I want to do that alone."

He looked into her determined face and still couldn't fathom walking out without her. "Let me worry about my future."

"My decision to stay is not only about you. As uncomfortable as it is, I have to face Keith and be honest."

How was he supposed to pretend for the rest of the night that he hadn't just made love to her? That she was going to leave Keith and be his, finally?

"Ransom, I'll meet you later. I promise."

He pulled her close and held her face in his hands. "I'm only doing what you ask. If you change your mind before the night is over, tell me, and we'll face him together."

"I will. Now go so I can fix my hair and get back out there."

Although he hated her request, Ransom did as she asked. But first, he pressed a firm kiss to her mouth, and quietly left.

Chapter Twenty-four

The minute Sophie saw Keith, guilt burned through her body. No amount of smoothing her hair and giving herself a pep talk could erase what she'd done in one of his parents' guest rooms.

"Where have you been?" Keith furrowed his brow at her.

"I went to get some fresh air for a few minutes." Her eyes dodged his.

He studied her with an unusual amount of concentration, his eyes scouring her face. "Are you okay?" he asked.

"Yes. Why?" Her heart raced.

"You look flushed." Using a forefinger, he tilted up her chin and searched her eyes.

"I'm fine." Sophie swallowed, insides quivering at the intense scrutiny.

"You're shaking."

Apparently her outside was quivering as well.

"No, I'm not." She denied the accusation with a straight face, a dull and emotionless tone to her voice.

His eyes focused on her mouth. "Your lipstick is gone."

"Is it? I'll have to go to the bathroom and freshen up." She'd left her purse in this room and hadn't been able to reapply the red lipstick. Her mouth still felt swollen and achy from Ransom's kisses.

Keith dropped his hand and scanned the room, gaze moving slowly from person to person. Searching. "Where's Ransom?"

"I don't know. I don't keep up with him."

His eyes snapped back to her and his mouth tightened a fraction. "I never said you did."

She'd said too much. Her guilty conscience would give her away.

Keith took her hand and held it unusually tight. "I messed up in the past, but I love you, Sophie. I plan to make it up to you, for everything I did. I'm not the same man I used to be."

"I know. I see the change in you."

She did. He was different, more considerate, and took time out of his schedule to spend with her, and not once had he cancelled a date—but the changes had come too late. Being inconsiderate and cheating on her created an opening, and another man slipped through.

He ran his thumb back and forth over the back of her hand. "Good. I want you to keep an open mind about us and not let anything…or anyone interfere."

Her cheeks burned. Was he warning her or accusing her? She couldn't be certain.

"I have a few more people to introduce you to," Keith said, placing his hand at the small of her back.

They walked toward a small group that included his mother and Myriam, and that's when she finally saw Ransom, in a corner of the room, watching them.

****

Ransom had slipped back into the party before Sophie and kept watch for her at the door. Seeing her so soon after they'd made love and not being able to touch her filled him with frustration. He began to doubt he'd made the right decision by allowing her to dictate the way the night ended.

"Ransom."

A clap on his shoulder drew his attention.

Brit smiled at him. "Enjoying yourself?"

He swirled the glass of cognac that he hadn't taken a sip of yet. He didn't know if he could eat or drink until he saw Sophie later tonight. "Absolutely."

"We're very impressed with your handling of the Creplar case. The client was ecstatic that we were able to settle for such a reasonable amount."

"The extenuating circumstances helped."

"Certainly." Brit laughed. "You've been doing an excellent job—better than excellent the past few years. Where do you see yourself in five years?"

The answer should be easy, but suddenly wasn't. Ransom's thoughts veered toward the restaurant plans on his computer. He thought, too, about his brother and his family in the suburbs. Tonight they were probably engaging in a simple activity, like watching TV in the family room, Ryker and Madison bouncing around and climbing all over Ryan. Later, when the kids were asleep, he and Shawna would finally have some time alone to cuddle and talk and dream.

"Ransom?"

His attention jerked back to Brit.

"In five years, I expect to be in a managing partner position. That's the ultimate goal."

Pleased with the answer, Brit smiled easily. "I'm sure that's in your future. A few of us are going into my lair to smoke cigars. Do you smoke?"

An invitation into Brit's private sanctuary was almost unheard of, but considered the ultimate invitation. Not everyone present here tonight would receive the same invite.

"I have on occasion," Ransom replied.

"Wonderful. Follow me."

He followed behind Brit, his eyes briefly meeting Sophie's. The corners of her mouth lifted softly, encouragingly, and he exited the room, marching forward to his destiny.

Chapter Twenty-five

Keith waited for her in the bedroom, yet Sophie sat in the bathroom on the toilet cover, wiping at her leaking eyes. Ever since the party ended, she'd been a mess of chaotic emotions. The room was a cloudy haze behind tears impossible to stop.

She was done, and she should tell him so. He deserved to know and not be strung along, but she feared the relationship-ending conversation, worried about upsetting him when he'd been trying so hard.

Sophie took a fortifying breath to calm her queasy stomach. She couldn't stay in here all night. She had to face him at some point.

At the sink, she splashed water on her face. Staring at her reflection, she saw a woman who was worried but resolved. Fearful, but ready to be honest. She exited the bathroom to find Keith standing at the window. He turned when he heard her come out of the room.

Sophie went to sit at the foot of the bed, and he walked over, pushing up the shirtsleeves on his arms.

"Are you okay? You were in there for a while." He spoke in a library whisper, concern etched into his wrinkled brow.

Sophie breathed slowly and quietly out of her mouth, heart pounding. "I can't do this anymore."

His body stilled, and she didn't think it was possible, but the room actually became quieter. If a feather dropped on the plush carpet, she was certain she'd hear it.

"Do what?" he asked slowly.

"Us. I can't keep up the pretense." Her voice wobbled from the weight of regret and the pain she would cause.

Anger laced his features. "That's what you've been doing with me all this time? Pretending?"

"Yes," she said quietly.

"Should I be embarrassed or upset?"

"I can't tell you how to feel."

His chest lifted as he breathed in deeply, and lowered on a loud exhale. "I'm sorry I said what I did about your profession as a flight attendant. I didn't mean it."

"Your comments about my job aren't the reason we don't work."

"Then explain why we don't work." Frustration and hurt vibrated in his voice.

Tears sprang to Sophie's eyes because she understood she was the one causing the anger. She was the one inflicting the pain.

"We're fighting a losing battle."

Her feelings for Keith had slowly shriveled and teetered on the edge of suffocation. No matter how much she tried to breathe life into them, the damage was done. The only time she truly felt excitement was with Ransom. The only arms she longed to be in were his.

"What will it take for you to forgive me and make this work?" Keith dropped to his haunches before her and rested his hands on her knees. "You haven't given us enough time, and that's what you need to do. That's what you promised you'd do."

"I know what I promised."

"Then do it!"

She covered her face. "I *can't*. I know what I promised, but I can't. Time won't change how I feel." She lowered her hands and looked him in the eyes. He deserved to be looked in the eyes. No matter what had happened between them, she didn't want to lie and deceive him. She knew what that felt like. "I—I did something—"

"*No.*" His voice and shoulders went taut at the same time. His eyes dropped to the carpet. "I don't care. I don't want to know. Whatever you did doesn't matter."

"It does matter."

"Not to me." He looked up at her, pain in his eyes, gripping her thighs.

Oh god, he knew. He knew there was something between her and Ransom, but never said a word. The knowledge ripped a hole in her heart. Was his decision to ignore the truth an act of love or complacency?

"I want to be honest."

"I don't want your honesty. I want...I want you, Sophie. I fucked up so many times in the past, and I know I didn't treat you the way you deserved. I *know*.

Just give it time. We can fix this."

"No," she whispered. "We can't. It's too late."

She wiped away another round of tears and sniffled. "I loved you. I just...don't l-love you anymore." Her voice cracked on the sentence, and he flinched.

She'd loved him, truly and deeply, but sitting here in the painful moment that signaled the end of their relationship, she could no longer recall how or why she fell for him in the first place. Staying with him, loving him, had become an act of desperation. She'd held on long past the expiration date because she didn't want the life of so many other women— successful in their careers, but unhappy in love and alone.

"You never forgave me for cheating on you."

"Your cheating was not the only reason for our problems, and you know that. Our relationship was in trouble for a long time, but the cheating was the last straw. The truth is, I did forgive you, but...everything has changed. We're not the same. I'm not the same. I'm no longer satisfied." Not when she knew there was a better alternative.

To her shame, she'd tolerated the disappointments in the relationship simply because she didn't want to be alone. She hadn't understood there was nothing wrong with being alone, and that being alone didn't have to mean being lonely.

Dropping his shoulders, Keith closed his eyes. His head fell onto her lap, an expression of utter and complete defeat on his face. She'd never seen Keith like this before. The sight of his pain wounded her because she had loved him at one time, and a small part of her even wished she could still love him to save them both the agony of separation.

She ran a hand over his black hair. "I'm sorry."

He sighed and stood abruptly, his features hardened into fierce, proud lines, but she still saw the hurt in his eyes. "He's not any better than I am. Mark my words, you're going from the frying pan into the fire. I'm willing to give you everything your heart desires to hold on to you, but you want mediocre. You're willing to settle."

Sophie mulled the accusation and came to an enlightened answer. "That's where you're wrong. I'm not willing to settle. Not anymore."

****

Ransom paced the apartment, his body bursting with energy, anxiety radiating in his aching shoulders.

Every time he called Sophie's phone, it went straight to voicemail. Was she with Keith? Had she changed her mind and lay his bed now, right after she and Ransom had been intimate and she'd trembled to completion in his arms?

The thought cut through him, and he snatched up the phone one more time to try to reach her. When the call went to voicemail again, he slammed the phone on top of the kitchen bar. Pounding, pounding until it splintered into pieces that flew across the marble and onto the tile floor.

Damn. He'd destroyed another phone.

He stared at the parts, chest heaving, fingers clenched into a fist. He *needed* to talk to her.

A loud rap on the door jolted his head up. Could it be...?

He rushed across the floor and flung open the

door.

A fist flew in and slammed into his cheek. Dizzying pain burst across the left side of his face, and Ransom fell backward onto the hardwood floor, landing hard on his tailbone. Pain shot up his spine and he shook his head to shake off the disorienting nature of the surprise attack.

Cupping his cheek, he looked up through the haze at Keith standing in the doorway, rubbing the hand he'd used as a battering ram. "You better take care of her."

What the hell?

The punch and the words had to be about Sophie. No doubt about it.

Ransom was going to kill him.

He surged to his feet and barreled toward Keith, shoulders low in a football tackle, and slammed him into the opposite wall. He followed up with two quick jabs to the abs and Keith jackknifed at the waist.

Ransom didn't waste any time slamming a tight fist to Keith's jaw, knocking him facedown into the carpeted corridor. Vibrating with anger, Ransom stood over him. Keith moaned on the floor, clutching his face.

In the distance, the elevator chimed.

"Where is she?" Ransom asked between gritted teeth.

"Fuck you," Keith said. He spat blood and rolled onto his hands and knees.

"Where. Is. She?"

"Ransom!"

His head jerked up at the sound of Sophie's shrill voice. Her gaze swung between the two of them.

Ransom rushed toward her, but she took two steps

back, eyes wide. Tentatively, she touched his throbbing cheek, her fingertips cool and comforting on his burning skin. "Your face."

"I'm fine." He covered her hand with his. He never wanted to let her go.

Keith struggled to his feet. Using the wall to prop himself up, he swiped blood from his mouth with the back of his hand. "Couldn't wait to get over here, could you?" he asked Sophie. He didn't sound angry. He sounded...hurt. Defeated.

Ransom looped an arm around Sophie's shoulders and pulled her close to his side. "Get out of here, Keith."

When the younger man's gaze flicked to his, Ransom expected to see rage. Instead, he saw resignation. There was no more fight left in him. Keith slinked off down the hallway and left Ransom and Sophie alone.

"Come on." Ransom took her by the hand and pulled her into the apartment. "What happened between you and Keith?" he asked.

Sophie swallowed. "I broke up with him."

Ransom lifted her into a hard kiss. "You're mine now?" he muttered against her mouth.

"Yes," she breathed.

Hurriedly, they moved into the bedroom and stripped naked. They fell onto the cool sheets without another word, and Ransom pressed soft kisses into her breasts, licking at her sensitive nipples, sucking the turgid peaks as her delicate moans whispered in the dark room.

"Ransom." The way she said his name made his stomach quiver, both syllables sounding pained and raw as they trembled off her tongue.

He kissed her again, driving his tongue between her lips. Lips that belonged to him now. Lips that tasted so sweet he never wanted to stop kissing them.

Lacing their fingers together, he pulled her hands above her head and stretched his body over hers. He kissed her jaw and neck, even as his knee pried part her thighs and he pressed his hard length against her moist cleft.

Gasping, she arched upward, whispering his name again in a breathless plea.

He sank into her, groaning at the wet clasp that enveloped him. He had never felt this whole, this complete with any other woman. His eyes closed tight as he buried his face in her neck, dragging in lungfuls of air filled with the sweet jasmine aroma of her skin.

Her breathing fractured and legs lifted around his waist. He thrust his hips faster, in quick, hard succession, unable to stop the powerful drive of his body into her slick heat.

He felt the moment she came undone. Heard the broken cry issue from her throat. Felt her legs tighten and her internal muscles pulse around him.

Then he lost control, blood roaring in his ears. He released into her with backaching intensity, crushing the pillow on either side of her head, and shuddered, coming with such ferocity that for long moments he couldn't breathe, as if someone had turned off the oxygen in the room.

Sophie's soft arms enveloped him, and she kissed his jaw and the corner of his mouth. He rolled onto his side, pulling her with him into a mesh of arms and legs. She was soft and warm, and he didn't want to let go.

"I love you," she whispered, touching his cheek.

It was so natural. What else could be said after such an emotional coupling? The honesty and depth of feeling in her eyes was plain to see.

"I love you, too," he whispered back.

Chapter Twenty-six

Sophie and Brenda entered the Florida courtroom and sat behind Jay. His profile was grim, but when he saw them both, he smiled reassuringly, which Sophie knew was for Brenda's benefit. She put an arm around her friend's shoulders, and Brenda folded her hands tightly in her lap and sat stiffly on the wooden bench.

Across the room, Jenna sat with Dale, heads bent in conference with their attorneys.

"All rise!" the bailiff said. Everyone in the courtroom came to their feet. "Court is now in session. The Honorable Judge Jones is presiding."

The judge, a Caucasian woman whose wizened features and gray hair suggested she'd been presiding over court cases for decades, sat down.

"Please be seated."

The court proceedings went underway, and when Sophie was called to the stand, she testified to Jay's character and his relationship, as she had observed it, with the boys. Hours later they broke for lunch and Jay, Brenda, and Sophie stood in the hallway.

Jay rubbed a hand across the back of his neck. "Thank you for being here," he said to Sophie.

"Of course. Where else would I be? You guys are my friends and I want to see everything work out for you."

"It's not just about me," Jay said, his eyes earnest and face hardening in frustration. "Jenna and Dale should be thinking about the boys and what they want, but neither of them care about that."

Brenda rubbed a hand up and down her husband's arm. "Be patient."

"This has gone on long enough," Jay said.

Sophie's phone rang and she saw it was a call from Ransom. Only a month into their relationship, and every time she saw his number, her spirits soared. "I need to take this," she said. She walked away to a bay of windows near the bathroom at the end of the hall.

"How's it going?" Ransom asked.

She sighed. "I don't think this is going to go well for them. Jay doesn't want to drag the boys into this, but I think it might be his ace in the hole. The boys want to move in with him."

"Most people don't want to bring their kids into court proceedings. That's understandable. Not to mention, children are notoriously unreliable in a courtroom setting."

"So you're saying there's nothing my friends can do? There's got to be a solution that works in their favor." She wished she knew how to help them.

"In a situation like you described, the case can go either way. Both sides have a very compelling argument."

Sophie bit the inside of her cheek, watching as Brenda continued to provide comfort to Jay, rubbing his arm and speaking quietly to him. "Jenna's such a liar, though. She kept the paternity of one of the boys a secret. Shouldn't that count for something?"

"Not really. I don't practice family law, but I can tell you that the court will rule in the best interest of the children. She may have told a lie, but that doesn't make her a bad mother. The only way to forgo this process is if both parties come to an agreement."

"They're in court, so clearly they couldn't."

"Any chance Jenna will change her mind?"

"Let me put it this way. Any chance I'll be able to see you in five minutes, even though I'm in Florida and you're in Illinois?"

Ransom chuckled. "I'm just trying to help you out." His voice dropped. "On another note, if you want to have some phone sex…"

"No, I don't want phone sex," Sophie said, blushing. Outside the window, people walked briskly around the cement courtyard. "I'm standing in the middle of a courthouse."

"What color panties are you wearing?"

"Ransom." She bit her bottom lip.

"Just tell me the color."

She huffed with fake exasperation. "They're white."

"Lacy or plain?"

"I knew you wouldn't stop."

"Just tell me if they're lacy or not."

Sophie snuck a glance over her shoulder to make sure no one was nearby. "Plain white cotton. Seamless. Like the ones I wore the last time I saw you."

He groaned. "They fit your cute little ass so well."

"I have a big ass, thank you very much."

"Oh right, they fit your big ass so well."

"You're so full of shit." She smiled. "I want my panties back when I see you next time. And please wash them before you give them back."

"You'll never get them back, then."

"Ew. That's disgusting."

"I like to use them when I masturbate."

His lowered voice was making her horny. Whenever he talked like that, he always made her wet. "You use my dirty panties to masturbate?" she whispered.

"Since I can't have you."

Her fingers tightened around the phone. "You're a perv. And I'm so turned on right now."

He chuckled softly. "Hold on."

When Ransom put her on hold, Sophie let out a groan of irritation. She wanted him to continue talking dirty to her. Maybe she could slip into the bathroom and get him to finish, and then she could finger herself until she came. Phone sex made their long-distance relationship more tolerable.

She turned slightly, and that's when she saw Jenna slide past Jay and Brenda, tossing a furious glance in their direction. Her eyes landed on Sophie, and with a dismissive toss of her blond head, she entered the bathroom.

"I'm back. Sorry about that. One of the junior associates came into my office to ask a question. Where were we?"

"You know what, I have to go."

"What? I'm sporting a boner the size of a baton

here."

"Then you'll have to use that vivid imagination of yours to get yourself off. Or you can wait until I call you back and I explain what my mouth plans to do with that *baton* of yours."

He groaned. "You're an evil woman."

Sophie laughed, sagging against the wall. "I can't wait to see you this weekend."

"Me either."

"You'll be available, right?"

She hated sounding needy, but the last two times she'd flown to Chicago hadn't gone well. The first time, she arrived during the week, and Ransom stayed in the office until late. The second time she flew out on the weekend, only to have him leave for most of the day on Saturday because of an emergency with one of his clients, and they'd had to cancel their plans for dinner and a show. Sophie had expressed her disappointment, and he'd apologized profusely, but his behavior made her very uncomfortable, reminiscent of Keith's behavior before he changed.

"Those last couple of times couldn't be helped. I promise things will be better. We'll go to dinner on Friday night and a bike ride on Saturday."

She smiled, relieved. "Perfect. I'll call you later."

After hanging up, Sophie marched into the bathroom and waited in front of the sinks until Jenna came out.

The blonde stopped in her tracks and eyed her warily. "What do you want?" she asked.

"To talk. That's it."

"Well, I don't want to talk to you. I know whose side you're on." She moved stiffly over to the sink.

"Are you proud of yourself?" Sophie asked.

Jenna ignored her, squirting soap into her palm.

"I know why you're doing this, and it's ridiculous."

Jenna snapped her head in Sophie's direction. "It's ridiculous to want my kids? It's ridiculous to not want to split up my sons? You know nothing about being a mother." She twisted on the water with a vengeance.

"You're right, but I know what it's like to be jealous, angry, and hurt. All of those emotions lead people to make bad decisions."

Under the running water, Jenna rubbed her hands together with much more force than necessary. "I don't think I need to take advice from someone who lets men walk all over her."

The cutting barb landed with the right dose of vitriol and jabbed Sophie in the gut. Their eyes met in the mirror, and Sophie saw the malevolence in her ex-friend's face, but she persevered.

"The court battle isn't about your kids and you know it. You're upset about Jay and Brenda."

Jenna tugged off a paper towel. "You're friends. So why should I listen to anything you have to say?" She dried her hands, tossed the paper, and placed a fist on her hip.

Sophie saw Jenna's behavior for what it was—posturing. She was hurting. She was embarrassed, and if she didn't acknowledge her behavior now, even more people would get hurt.

"You and Jay had an agreement. The boys would stay with him starting in the fall, and all three have been looking forward to it. They want to stay with their dad."

"Marco is not his son."

"But Jay is the only father he's known. And to Jay, he *is* his son."

"That doesn't change anything. Dale has a right to spend time with his son."

"You and I both know Jay would never keep Marco from him. That's not the kind of man he is. He's the kind of man who discovered one of his sons is not his, and he wants to be there for him emotionally and financially. He wants to raise him. Despite his anger and hurt, his love for Marco has not changed one iota."

Jenna swallowed and stared at the floor.

"Dale will probably go along with whatever you decide, so why drag everyone through the trial? So you can punish Jay for falling in love with Brenda? So you can punish Brenda for being with a man you don't even want anymore—you just don't want her to have him?"

Jenna remained silent and kept her gaze glued to the tiled floor. Sophie saw that as a good sign. "How much more hurt has to be doled out to make you happy? Enough already." Now that she was on a roll, she couldn't stop. The words poured out of her. "For years you've been getting your revenge, but you're not just hurting Brenda and Jay. You're hurting yourself, your kids, and everyone around you. Stop the games. Do the right thing and end this."

Sophie reached for her former friend, but Jenna pulled back. The enmity had disappeared from Jenna's eyes, but her lips formed into a hard line.

"Do yourself, Jay, and Brenda a favor. Mind your own business, Sophie." She stalked out.

Sophie sighed, gnawing on her lip, and hoping she hadn't done more harm than good.

****

Ransom signed the last of the contracts and rubbed a hand down his face. Glancing at his watch, he decided to take the last few minutes to make preparations for Sophie's visit this weekend. After messing up the last couple of times she came to see him, he couldn't afford to again. Based on their conversation, her patience was wearing thin.

He made reservations for dinner at The Signature Room at the 95th, atop the John Hancock building on Michigan Avenue. They didn't have many vegetarian options, but after a short call he learned they could accommodate Sophie's diet with a vegetable lasagna they served at lunch, or the chef would be happy to prepare one of the other entrees as a vegetarian meal.

He then ordered snacks and prepared foods to keep on hand from a local vegetarian and vegan place he recently discovered. She was always checking labels, and he'd become more conscious of ingredients as a result. Just the other day, he chewed out the owner of a deli for making vegetable soup with chicken stock, something he would never have paid attention to before if not for Sophie.

Twiddling the pen between his fingers, Ransom flipped through a couple of pages on his desk calendar. Maybe they should take a trip together…

At a short rap on the door, he lifted his head. "Come in."

Giles sauntered in, hands tucked in the pockets of his slacks. "How's it going?"

"Great. How's it going with you? Still happily married?"

"Of course."

"I guess Stephanie's the one I should ask that

question to, right?"

"Ha-ha, you're hilarious. What are you up to?" Giles walked over to the desk.

Ransom rubbed his jaw. "Looking to see when I could take a week or two off."

"You're going on a vacation?" Giles asked in an incredulous voice.

"Thinking about it. I'm overdue." Ransom shrugged.

Rolling onto the balls of his feet, Giles remarked, "You know, everyone's been talking about you and your behavior lately."

"My behavior?" Ransom said, tilting back the chair. *This should be interesting.* "What are you talking about?"

"You don't even realize how much you've changed, do you? You're a different man. No more frowning face. You're whistling in the halls. I saw you come in from lunch, and you smiled at a junior attorney. *Smiled.* He turned around to stare after you in confusion."

"You're exaggerating," Ransom said with a chuckle.

Giles pointed at him. "See, that's what I'm talking about. You're laughing, *a lot.* Sophie's been good for you."

"I'm not going to argue. She has been good for me." He loved her and every little thing about her.

He couldn't get enough of the fall of her hair as they lay in bed together, sweeping over his arm and the pillow. He'd been attracted to her voice from the moment they met, and that hadn't changed. Her constant chatter was a soothing backdrop to the chaos of his life, like the hum of a TV or music coming from a radio's speakers. He didn't always pay attention to what she was saying, and every now and again she'd stop and say, "Are you listening?" The truth was, he might not be, but he'd say yes, and she'd start right back up again, telling her story, and he'd fall back into that easy, comfortable peace that she brought about in him.

When they used FaceTime that was simply a bonus. Then he had the pleasure of seeing her radiant smile and colorful clothes, which always lifted his spirits no matter what type of day he'd had.

Giles folded his arms over his chest. "Don't tell me The Shark has lost his teeth. I never—"

Brit appeared in the doorway, and Ransom and Giles straightened immediately. Brit Wong never deigned to enter the office of lowly associates.

"Brit," Giles said.

The older man returned the greeting with a perfunctory nod before turning to Ransom. "I wondered if I could have a word with you."

"Sure." Ransom glanced at Giles.

"I was just on my way out," his friend said. "I'll talk to you later."

Behind Brit's back, Giles's eyes went wide, and he shot a *holy shit* face at Ransom before closing the door.

Brit sat in a chair and folded one leg over the other. "I don't think I've ever been in your office before."

He inspected the room, while Ransom's abdomen tightened into a wall of cement. Since fighting with Keith, he'd been expecting some kind of retaliation and dreading this day, wondering when it would come, though he never expected Brit to come to him.

He expected a summons to his office.

Brit brushed nonexistent lint from his immaculate pant leg. "I've been meaning to talk to you for some time." In true Brit fashion, he didn't beat around the bush. Resting his elbows on the armrests of the chair, he steepled his fingers. "I've watched you since you came to the firm. I knew you would be a great asset for us, and you have been. Which is why when my son came to me with a delicate situation concerning you and his now ex-girlfriend, I chose instead to give him a stern talking to."

Ransom remained silent, clenching his jaw as he awaited the rest of Brit's speech.

"I'm well aware that my son has made some bad decisions over the years. He can be a bit self-centered, but at the core, he's a good person. He's my son, and I love him. But I'm a practical man. I run a highly profitable business, and I was not about to let go of one of my best assets because of his hurt feelings."

Brit studied him over his fingers, and Ransom waited with a stomach so tangled up in nerves, he felt nauseated. There was more, and he suspected the rest would be much, much worse than Keith running to his father with hurt feelings.

"However, there are cameras all over my house. Not for spying, but as a precautionary measure. One can't be too careful. I never even look at the footage unless there's a need to. Without going into detail, recently there was a need to, and I discovered something that I'm sure my son is not aware of, nor do I plan to tell him. The night of the cocktail party, a camera in the hall recorded you and Keith's date, Miss Bradshaw, entering a bedroom."

Shit.

Ransom's heart rate sped up and pounded a loud, vicious beat in his chest and skull. "Brit, I can—"

Brit lifted a hand. "The reason for this conversation is not to get an explanation. I don't care about your explanation. The reason for this conversation is to tell you that you made a mistake that night. You used poor judgment. Top associates do not use poor judgment. However..." He smiled, but the smile didn't reach his eyes. "As I mentioned before, I'm a practical man, and I believe everyone should be allowed to make one mistake. After all, no one is perfect, and I'm certain there will be no more poor decision-making from such an important member of our team."

The pounding in his skull abated somewhat. "That's correct."

"Excellent. That's what I thought." Brit rose from the chair and left. He didn't say goodbye. He didn't look over his shoulder. He just walked out.

Shit, shit, shit.

Ransom slumped in the chair and rubbed his pounding head. He was too close to fuck up now. Moving forward, he'd have to be a lot more careful.

Chapter Twenty-seven

"Ladies and gentlemen, on behalf of the Noble Airlines crew, we welcome you to Midway International Airport in the city of Chicago. The temperature is seventy degrees Fahrenheit, twenty-one degrees Celsius. We would like to thank you for joining us on this trip and we're looking forward to seeing you on board again in the near future. Enjoy your stay!"

Sophie replaced the microphone and she and the other flight attendants said goodbye to the passengers as they disembarked. After conducting post-landing tasks, they walked into the terminal.

"Where are you headed?" Jalinda asked as she pulled along her carry-on. They hadn't seen each other since the trip to the Bahamas, but had wound up on the same flight again.

Sophie walked briskly beside her, dragging her own wheeled luggage. "To see my boyfriend. You?"

"Parents. I have a few extra days, and I'm pretty sure they're going to plan all manner of activities that involve setting me up with their friends' sons because they want me to settle down." She rolled her eyes.

"My parents don't bother."

"Because you're smart and got yourself a man before they could interfere."

They entered the employee area and performed the usual checklist of activities before parting ways. Sophie dialed Ransom's number on the way out of the terminal.

When the voicemail picked up, she said, "Hey, I'm on the way and I'm starving. See you in a bit."

They were going to the John Hancock building for dinner. She bit down on a grin. As many times as she'd been to Chicago, she'd never set foot inside the iconic skyscraper. The views from the top were supposed to be extraordinary, and dinner at the restaurant among the best in the city.

Sophie arrived at Ransom's swanky high-rise building, nodded to the guard, and took a seat on one of the soft gray chairs crowded around a low table in the lobby. While she waited, she checked email and sent a text to her parents.

Then she waited some more.

Brenda called and shared great news. "Jenna agreed to let both of the boys move to Atlanta!" she screamed, crying at the same time.

Sophie gasped. "She did?"

"Yes! We're still in Florida because they were due back in court on Monday, but out of the blue, Jenna called this morning and said she wanted to work things out. We just got back from a meeting with her and Dale, and I had to call and give you the good news." Brenda sniffed. "Visitation has been worked out to make sure Dale gets to see his son as often as he can. We're going to put everything in writing, of course, but it's over, Sophie. All the angst and stress is finally at an end."

They both squealed into the phone.

"I'm so happy for you and Jay," Sophie said, tears of joy filling her eyes.

"Thank you, honey. And thank you for being there for us. We'll see you when we get back."

Sophie hung up, spirits lifted and a huge smile on her face.

She checked the time on her phone. Ransom was late. Thirty minutes late at this point. She uncrossed and recrossed her legs, staring at the revolving door.

A dark-haired woman about her age walked in and went to the elevators.

Sophie shifted in the chair.

Another fifteen minutes passed.

The elevator dinged and a couple exited, marched across the shiny floor, and went into the street.

Sophie stared down at her phone. No missed calls. No voicemail message. No texts.

She sent a text.

Where are you?

She waited.

Almost an hour and forty-five minutes later, Ransom rushed in, briefcase in hand, dressed to impress in a dark suit and skinny charcoal tie. He walked past the guard desk with long strides and came to stand in front of her.

Sophie stood, arms crossed. "You're late. You told me you'd be here by six. You didn't even call."

"I apologize, but it was unexpected." He sounded

irritated, as if she'd done something wrong.

"If I could be on time, so could you. Showing up almost two hours late is unacceptable."

"Damn it, Sophie, can we not have this conversation here and now?" He grabbed the handle of her luggage and walked away, not even waiting to make sure she followed.

But she did follow. She stepped into the elevator and stood in the farthest corner, away from him.

"I'm one of the best lawyers in the firm," Ransom said when the doors closed. "The drawback is that everyone wants a piece of me, and when there's a problem, I'm the one they call."

Sophie stared straight ahead.

"It couldn't be helped," he added.

She kept quiet and heard him sigh.

They went down the hall to his condo, a contemporary-designed space decorated in black and white and neutral tans.

Sophie stood in the middle of the floor and crossed her arms. "I'm only here until Sunday." They were supposed to spend time together and had already lost two hours.

Ransom tossed off his jacket. "I know. We missed our reservation at the restaurant, but we can still do something. There are plenty of places within walking distance."

"Are you listening to yourself? You completely screw up our evening out and you try to pacify me with a sorry substitute. I was looking forward to going to the Signature Room because I've never been to the John Hancock building. It would have been a nice night out for us."

"Sophie, I'm sorry."

"Where were you?"

"One of the partners called me into a meeting. I couldn't exactly turn him down. They want me to be a consultant for a company in Texas. It'll mean a lot of money for the firm."

"And another prestigious assignment for you."

"Yes. There's nothing wrong with that."

"Have you even been working on your restaurant idea?"

"You and the damn restaurant. That's all you talk about anymore. I'm an attorney, not a chef. This is what I do. I went to school to practice law." He let out a puff of air. "I don't want to fight."

"Then you should have been here on time." She took a good look at him and didn't like what she saw. She could practically interchange his face with Keith's, their behavior was so similar.

"You want me to change overnight and it's not that easy," he said in a heavy tone.

"Not if you're not trying."

"I am trying!"

"No, you're not! You asked me what I wanted, and I told you, but you're not going to change, and I was foolish enough to think that you could make time in your busy schedule for me."

"You're being ridiculous." He tugged on his tie and walked away from her toward the kitchen.

"No, I'm not," Sophie said, following him.

He whirled on her. "You knew the kind of man I was when you met me. I've always been upfront about who I am. I work hard. My time is limited. I'm doing the best I can, but I can't drop everything to play house with you."

"Play house with me?" She laughed shrilly.

"People make time for the things they want. For having babies. For starting a business. For treating your girlfriend like she's more than a damn afterthought. There's never a right time to do anything, so you do it now. When you feel it. When you want it. You're missing out on life. On living. On doing."

"It's so easy for you to judge. You don't have my responsibilities and you've never had anyone look down their nose at you and predict that you'll never amount to anything because you made some mistakes when you were young."

The room went silent.

A muscle in his jaw flexed. "And yes, I know it's in the past," he said.

But not so far in the past that he had forgotten.

"So you're just going to keep living this...this life that you no longer enjoy, when the one you want is within reach? But because it's not prestigious enough for you to rub in the faces of the people that put you down, you're willing to sacrifice your own happiness? Do you know how ridiculous it is to work so hard to impress other people at the expense of your own happiness?"

He frowned at her. "You think you're so much smarter and better than everyone else because you *chose* to be a flight attendant. I'm ecstatic for you, but some people want more in life."

"Yes, I chose to become a flight attendant, and I love it. I'm passionate about people and love to travel. Passion, Ransom. Do you remember our conversation? What are you passionate about? What do you choose to do, except hide behind a law degree doing work you don't even enjoy, instead of what you're passionate about? Don't stand there and judge me, when you're not even being true to yourself."

"I am true to myself! This is what I want. This condo. These things. This suit." He yanked off the tie. "My car. Everything. So I'm late a few times or have to cancel a few events. If you loved me the way you say you do, you wouldn't try to change me. You'd be more understanding."

Sophie laughed softly to herself, shaking her head. "From the frying pan into the fire."

"What?" he asked sharply.

"It's only going to get worse once you become partner, isn't it?"

"We don't know that. Just give me a little more time. I'm so close. You know how important this is to me."

"I know." *More important than me.* "But you're not even happy."

"Happiness is overrated."

That had to be one of the saddest things she'd ever heard, and he didn't even understand how dismal saying something like that was.

Ransom scrubbed a hand across his forehead. "I'm sorry. Just give me a little more time."

He sounded exhausted, but she was done being treated as an afterthought. There would always be something else taking priority, and she couldn't hold on anymore. She wanted to be the priority.

"How about this," she said quietly. "You don't have time for me. I don't have time for you."

She walked over to her luggage.

"Sophie, it won't happen again."

"Damn right it won't."

"What does that mean? What the fuck are you

doing? Put down the bag."

She picked up her purse.

"Sophie."

No matter how much she loved Ransom, she had to walk away. She'd been in this position before—for three years—and promised herself she'd never do it again. She couldn't. It damaged her self-worth.

She went to the door with her belongings, but Ransom yanked away the suitcase. "You're not going anywhere."

"Leave me alone. I'm not doing this with you."

"You're overreacting."

"Give me my suitcase." She reached for the luggage but he held it out of reach. "Stop!"

She hit him in the chest with a fist, and he grabbed her arms and slammed her back against the wall.

They were both breathing hard, emotion and energy filling the air.

His fingers bit into the soft flesh of her arms. "Don't leave me."

The words tore at her heart. "I don't have a choice. Just let me go."

He didn't budge.

"Please," she whispered.

He collapsed against her, pressing his face into her neck. "Sophie."

She rested her cheek against his. "I can't do it. Not again," she whispered.

As he lifted his head, his thumbs rubbed the spots where he'd squeezed her arms. "I can't walk away."

"I'm not asking you to. I'm walking away."

He turned his mouth toward hers, but she twisted away from the kiss. "Let's not make this any harder. Chemistry is not enough. We made a mistake thinking that it was."

He stood in place for a little bit longer, but she kept her eyes averted. Finally, he moved aside, and on wobbly legs she walked over to take the handle of the suitcase. Her chest hurt as she stepped to the door, expecting him to say that she deserved better treatment.

She kept hoping he would stop her, but he never did. Not when she crossed the floor. Not when she exited the door. Not when she entered the elevator.

By the time she was seated in the back of the taxi on the way to a hotel, she finally accepted that he wouldn't.

Chapter Twenty-eight

Sophie flew back to Atlanta early the next day, but instead of going home, she drove to her parents' house. She parked her Jeep in the driveway, and before she could even knock, her mother opened the door and pulled her into her arms.

Tears flooded her eyes as they sat on the sofa, her mother cradling her head against her chest.

"Was I wrong?" Sophie sniffled. Perhaps watching couples like her parents and Brenda and Jay had skewed her perception of relationships.

Dora touched her with soothing strokes to her hair. "Absolutely not. You don't deserve to be treated like that."

From the corner of her eye, she saw her father's feet appear at the entrance to the room, checking on them. Her mother gestured at him, and he walked back out.

"Relationships are tough, and they require time

and energy to nurture and grow. Both people have to be invested." Her mother petted her hair. "I never told you this, but your father and I didn't always have a perfect relationship."

Sophie lifted her head. "I can't believe the two of you ever had problems."

"In the beginning, it was rough. Your father never took me anywhere, and I finally figured out it was because I was white."

Sophie gasped. "You never told me that."

"Well, imagine back then, a dreadlocked man, serious about the advancement of his race, working toward a doctorate in African-American studies, talking about the Motherland and black love, had fallen in love with a white woman. You can understand his dilemma." She chuckled softly. "I can laugh about it now, but my goodness, it hurt like the dickens. He convinced me to keep our relationship a secret for a long time, but not just because of our families. Because he worried about what people would think. I finally put my foot down. I told him if he didn't want to be seen with me, then I'd move on to someone who wasn't embarrassed to be seen in public with me. I was terrified he would let me go."

"But he didn't," Sophie said softly.

"He did a complete one-eighty. He chose me and made sure *everybody* knew we were together. He received some pushback from his friends, and of course there was the problem with our families, but our relationship changed drastically. Adversity only made it stronger. He took me everywhere, held my hand, introduced me as his girlfriend, and couldn't keep his hands off of me in public. Still can't. He's always holding my hand or giving me a kiss." She smiled, her eyes glowing with happiness. She laid a hand against Sophie's cheek and gazed into her eyes. "I said all of that to say, sometimes you have to put your foot down, sweetie. The result may not be what you want, but you don't deserve to be treated as if your feelings don't matter, as if you're nothing more than an afterthought. Not by anyone, and certainly not by someone who claims to love you. Your feelings matter. Your heart matters."

Sophie sniffed. "It's hard to let go, though."

"I know." Dora stroked her hair. "But when a man really cares about you, he makes an effort, not an excuse."

Sophie rested her head on her mother's shoulder again. "I sure know how to pick 'em."

"I'm confident one of these days you'll find a man who sees you for the jewel you are. For some women, it happens later than others. But he's out there, sweetie. You just have to be patient. When you find him, you'll know. Because he'll choose you."

****

Ransom drummed his fingers against the desk, thinking long and hard about the case before him. He was almost certain the plaintiff was lying about his client, and he needed to prove it. But how?

Sophie.

Dammit! He pinched the bridge of his nose.

He couldn't concentrate for thinking about her. He'd called several times since she left, but each time she sent his call to voicemail and simply texted back that she was busy.

A sound at the door caused him to lift his head,

relieved at the distraction. His assistant, Lena, stood before him, a little breathless, eyes overly bright behind blue frames that matched her blue pantsuit.

Ransom lowered the documents he'd been reading onto the desk. "What's wrong, and what are you still doing here?" It was an hour past the time she usually left work.

She waved her hand dismissively. "I had some filing to do and thought I'd stay behind and get it taken care of instead of waiting until tomorrow." She took a deep breath. "Mr. Wong saw me when I was returning from making copies and stopped me with a message for you." A dramatic pause. "He and the other partners would like to see you in his office upstairs."

"Now?" Ransom jumped to his feet, his heart kicking up several notches at the implication in her words. "Did he say why?"

She shook her head briskly. "Not even a hint of what it was about," she said, but the broad smile on her face indicated she had her suspicions.

He lifted his jacket from the coat rack and buttoned it. Lena dusted off his shoulders and straightened his tie. "Congratulations, sir."

Ransom clenched his fists to offset the nervous energy channeling through his body. "There's no guarantee. There could be any number of reasons why they want to see me."

"Right," Lena said, bouncing with excitement.

Ransom breathed quietly through his lips and squared his shoulders. If his prescient assistant thought this was his moment, then it was. "I better get up there."

With Lena's broad grin and a thumbs-up sign

pushing him forward, Ransom exited his office and took the elevator to the top floor.

The moment he'd been dreaming about since he took his first law class was now upon him. He knew it. All his hard work, dedication, and sacrifice would finally pay off. Exiting the elevator, his steps faltered on the way to Brit Wong's office.

He stood in the middle of the carpeted outer office, the silence ominous and oppressive. He wanted this. He did. But now that the moment was upon him, he felt a slight hesitation. A niggling doubt in a corner of his brain.

He *did* want this.

Sophie had gotten inside his head, and now he questioned everything he had ever wanted professionally. Ransom fisted his hands and marched forward, shoving aside Sophie's accusations, Sophie's smiles, and Sophie's sweet nature. Yes, he missed her. He'd hardly been able to sleep for thinking about her, but she expected him to walk away from all the hard work and trappings of the lifestyle he'd acquired. He needed someone supportive by his side. Someone who understood his needs.

He arrived at the double doors that led into Brit's office and knocked, and on the inside, Brit called for him to enter.

The founding member and four of the managing partners were seated on the leather sofas, each of them holding a cigar and a glass of ruby-colored port.

"Come on in." Brit waved him in with a wide smile.

What he wanted was assuredly in his reach within minutes, and he would not allow Sophie to make him doubt the course he'd been on for eleven years.

Ransom closed the doors, flashed a smile at the men, and prepared to accept the fruits of his labor.

Chapter Twenty-nine

Sophie pulled up outside the bike shop with the rest of the riders.

Eric parked his bike in front of the shop and hopped off. "Whew! That was awesome."

Sophie grinned as she lifted off her helmet. Rotating her shoulders, she said, "I couldn't agree more." Today had been a long ride on a new route that pushed her endurance, leaving her simultaneously exhausted and exhilarated.

"See you next week," Eric said, waving.

Sophie attached her bike to the back of the Jeep and strolled into her mother's juice shop. A few patrons occupied the tables, and her father stood behind the counter today, reviewing printouts of the new menus. Once again he'd used his graphic design skills to redesign them.

"I'm going home," she announced.

"Coming by for dinner on Monday?" her mother

asked, as she set a sack with smoothies atop the counter.

"Of course. I would be crazy to miss your zucchini." Her mother catered to Sophie's diet by having meatless Mondays and inviting her over whenever she was in town. Lengthwise sliced zucchini "boats" stuffed with quinoa, onions, cheese, and spinach was one of Sophie's favorite dishes.

She took the bag from the counter.

"Come here," her mother said, opening her arms.

Sophie groaned. "Dad, talk to her."

"Nobody can talk to your mother."

Sophie dragged over to her mother and allowed the embrace. "I'm fine," she muttered.

"I know, but I'm a mother. I worry." Dora squeezed tight and patted Sophie's back.

Her father held up two of the printouts. "Which one do you like better?" he asked.

Sophie tilted her head. "The one with more color, on the right."

"Definitely your mother's daughter," Walter said.

"And that's a good thing," Dora said firmly.

"All right, you two, I'm out of here. Ciao."

Sophie waved at her parents and walked out with the smoothies. In the Jeep, through the large window at the front of the store, she saw her mother playfully tugging on her father's dreadlocks. Walter pulled his wife closer by the waistband of her jeans, and they stayed attached to each other, poring over the options on the counter.

Yeah, they were cute. One day she'd have that.

Sophie left the shop, and on the way home, she called Brenda. "Hey, I won't be able to make it tonight," she said, driving south.

Brenda and Jay had invited her out for dinner to celebrate the arrival of Jay's boys in the fall.

"Why not? There'll be wine and plenty of food," Brenda said.

"Sorry, I'll have to pass."

"Come on, Sophie."

"I just had a long bike ride and all I want to do is take a nice warm bath and then read regulations manuals until I fall asleep."

The line went quiet. "Are you sure?"

"Yes, I'm sure."

She was also sure the only reason Brenda and Jay had come up with this so-called celebratory dinner was to make her feel better. Like her parents, they worried about her, and while she appreciated the concern, she didn't want to be coddled. Five weeks had already passed since her breakup with Ransom, and she'd gone through gallons of self-medication, courtesy of chocolate chip ice cream—the perfect cure for hurt feelings and broken hearts.

"Well...if you need me..."

"I know I can call you guys. Don't worry. And please don't drink wine while you're carrying my goddaughter."

"The wine was for you and Jay, silly. Take care. Call me if you need to, okay?" Her voice had dropped lower with concern.

"I will. I promise."

Sophie drove into her neighborhood, and the kids playing kickball in the street scattered. She pulled into her parking space and stepped down from the vehicle, and had walked through the breezeway to the door of her apartment when she realized she'd forgotten the smoothies. She turned around...and her heart stopped.

"Hi, Sophie."

The deep tenor made her knees weak. She hadn't heard his voice or seen his face in weeks because he'd stopped calling after only a few days.

Ransom looked heartbreakingly handsome, but in a different way than usual. He had a five o'clock shadow, and instead of one of his Armani suits or a pair of pressed slacks, he wore jeans hanging low on his hips and a blue V-necked T-shirt that exposed the muscles of his arms and the colorful ink extending down to the middle of his left forearm. He'd cut his hair in a classic undercut, short on the sides but long enough for her to trail her fingers through. The black titanium earring was back in his right ear, but though he appeared relaxed and at ease, there was an underlying tension in his stance.

"Why are you here?"

She didn't want to get too excited. She didn't want to believe that he was there for her. She'd been disappointed too many times, and the bruising on her heart at the most recent disappointment made her very tentative about how to receive him.

"Can you believe I was in the neighborhood?" he asked with a sideways smile. He came closer. "I had a million things I wanted to say to you. I had a speech all prepared where I'd convince you that we were meant to be and that I'd made a horrible mistake. I figured with flowery words I could convince you to take me back. I know it's been a long time, but that's what I want, Sophie. For you to look past my shortsightedness and mistakes and take me back."

"Why would I do that? I've been here before, and it never ends well for me." Her throat was tight. "We agreed that all we have is chemistry and we can't build a relationship on that alone."

"*We* didn't agree to that. You spoke and I remained silent."

"What are you saying?"

He took a deep breath. "That I love you, and I want another chance."

"This is all really nice, Ransom. If you'd come to me even a few weeks ago, my reaction might be different, but right now, I don't know how I feel. I've had a lot of time to think, and I just don't know that being with you is in my best interest right now. We're different. We want different things and have different goals. We live in different cities. It'll never work." Her heart broke a little bit with each addition to the list of reasons why they couldn't work.

"I left the firm."

She gasped. "What?" Surely she'd misunderstood him. Work was his life.

"They offered me the partnership, but I turned it down, turned in my two weeks' notice, and I left. My brother, of all people, called me impulsive and is certain I bumped my head. My parents think I'm nuts. But I've never felt more free."

"I'm wondering if you bumped your head, too," Sophie said.

He grinned, showing lots of teeth, his blue eyes sparkling, the dimples creating deep lines in his cheeks. She didn't think she'd ever seen him happier.

"I sold my car and put my condo up for sale. I had a contract in two weeks. I'll be flying back for the closing at the end of the month."

"I can't believe you did that. Where are you going to live now?"

"Atlanta."

Sophie's mouth fell open. "*Here?*" Her heart started a happy dance.

"I'm staying with my brother and his family until I find a place of my own. I flew in today and dropped off my things. Then I came here to wait for you."

"You've made some big decisions."

"That's not all. I've been working on my plan for the restaurant. I found a commercial realtor who'll help me find a place in a good location. I found someone to design the menus, and I've started interviewing contractors and architects." He grinned again. "I rented space in a commercial kitchen where I could practice. I'm hoping you're open to doing some taste-testing. After all, you're the one who insisted I should pursue my dream. My passion."

"I didn't say those things to make you—"

"You didn't make me do anything." He came to stand directly in front of her. "I'm here because I want to be. Because a stubborn, beautiful flight attendant gave me an ultimatum and made me face my fears and accept that I love her too much to lose her. She made me realize I was missing out on life because I was living my life for other people, and I'd never really be happy that way." He took her trembling hand in his and looked deeply into her eyes. "So if you don't mind an unemployed former attorney, I'm here. If you'll still have me."

She smiled, shaking her head in disbelief.

"You chose me." Her voice broke, and tears burned her eyes.

"There was no other choice." He lifted her hands to his lips and kissed the knuckles. "We're not doing this halfway. Sophie Bradshaw, will you be my wife, in sickness and in health, for richer, for poorer? Probably poorer. Much, much poorer. For as long as we both shall live?"

She laughed, her heart swelling with happiness. "That's completely impulsive, and it's crazy, and..."

"And...?" His hands tightened a fraction around hers, and his eyes kept her ensnared in the intensity of his gaze.

She couldn't torture him any longer. "And yes. Of course I'll marry you." Her smile was broad and happy. "Yes!"

She flung her arms around his neck and planted a big, wet kiss on his delicious lips.

Epilogue

Ransom came to sit beside Sophie on the sofa.

"Look at that pretty baby," she cooed at the computer screen.

In the living room back in Atlanta, Jay cradled his one-week-old daughter in his arms, turning her sleeping face to the camera. Wrapped in a yellow blanket with white polka dots, the baby slept soundly in her father's arms.

"The boys can't get enough of her," Brenda said beside him. "They've been helping me a lot. They feed her and even changed her diaper a couple of times."

"Lucky you, you have two nannies," Sophie said.

"Free child labor," Jay said with a chuckle.

"How are the boys adjusting?" Ransom asked.

"They still love it here," Jay answered. "Having each other for support helps. Arturo has joined the chess club, and they're both considering trying out for football next year. We'll see what happens."

"Well, I, for one, cannot wait to see my goddaughter in person," Sophie said.

"When are you coming back? Part of being a godmother is babysitting duties," Jay informed her.

Ransom looped his arm around her neck. "We may never come back."

Sophie leaned her soft body into his. "Don't listen to him. He has an appointment with someone on your creative team when we get back, plus he has a sit-down with the architect to go over the changes to the floor plan of the restaurant."

The plans for the restaurant were moving forward under the tentative name of The Hearty Kitchen, a farm-to-table restaurant. Ransom netted a hefty sum after the sale of his condo, and his real estate agent found commercial space in Midtown within his budget, an old house that needed work but was perfect for his restaurant idea. Coupled with a bank loan and money pledged from his brother and Sophie's father, he hoped to start renovations in a couple of months. In the meantime, he'd lucked out and purchased almost-new equipment from another restaurant closing, and had already received inquiries since advertising for a pastry chef and sommelier.

Being his own boss meant setting his own hours, and after discussing the long hours that restaurateurs often worked, he and Sophie agreed the restaurant would only serve dinner, Monday through Saturday.

Jay massaged Brenda's neck. "We're not going to keep you. She needs to rest. We'll see you when you get back."

Brenda smiled ruefully. "He's right, I'm exhausted. Samantha and Basil will be here in a few days to help out." Samantha was Brenda's mother, and Basil was her new husband. Their ceremony had been a huge party filled with friends and family—including Basil's children and Brenda's younger sister—and Ransom had gotten his first professional gig by catering the reception. "Thanks for calling," Brenda added.

"You took too long to send me the text," Sophie scolded.

"We didn't want to disturb you on your honeymoon, but I'll see you when you get back. Bye." Brenda blew them a kiss and waved at the screen.

The connection closed and Sophie got up from the sofa. "She looks tired but happy." She stretched her arms over her head. "Are we still going to the beach?"

They'd come back to where it all started—the Atlantis hotel on Paradise Island. They'd even splurged on a suite near the water, similar to the one Ransom had originally stayed in. Last night they ordered room service and sat out on the balcony, listening to the waves with Sophie's feet propped up on his lap as they discussed future plans.

"We are absolutely going to the beach," Ransom said, typing notes into the computer.

"I better take this off, then. I don't want it to get ruined in the salt water."

Ransom dragged his gaze from the computer screen and watched Sophie remove the conch shell and gold necklace and place it in the safe. It was the same one he'd bought for her birthday during their first visit. He'd held on to it the entire time and presented it to her the first night of their honeymoon—one of several gifts they exchanged during the course of the night.

She assembled the items they would need on the

beach while he typed rapidly, words flowing from his brain to his fingertips with more ideas. The passion and excitement was all there. Sometimes he lost track of time and space, and it was only when she quietly entered his office and suggested he take a break that he hung up the phone or tapped out the final words before getting up to eat.

She'd become his own personal food critic and design advisor. He often ran ideas by her that he had for the restaurant, and any new meatless dishes he wanted to try, she gave him honest, direct feedback. They didn't always agree, but he valued her opinion.

Ransom snapped the laptop closed. "I had to get that thought down before I forgot. All right, let's go. Chop, chop."

"Wait a minute, I'm coming."

Sophie donned her floppy hat and tossed sunscreen into the beach bag. "Now I'm ready."

Standing at the door, Ransom looked down at his wife. Her happiness and zest for life made him see what his life could be. How did he get so lucky?

"Seeing Brenda and Jay with their newborn, and Ryan and Shawna with their new son, makes me think more and more about having kids."

"Are you saying you're ready?" Sophie asked. No one could miss the note of excitement in her voice.

"Yeah. Why wait?"

"I agree."

"And think of all the fun we'll have as we try to get pregnant," Ransom said, wiggling his brows.

Sophie giggled and dragged his head down to hers for a kiss, smiling into his eyes. Her lips tasted like they always did—sweet and soft, and utterly intoxicating.

"Let's go, Mr. Stewart."

They left the room hand in hand. As they walked toward the beach, Ransom felt as if he floated on air. If someone had told him that on his first trip to the Bahamas he would find a fulfilling relationship and be married less than a year later, he would have scoffed at the absurdity of the prediction.

Maybe it was luck. Maybe it was timing. But he'd found a relationship where each partner treated the other as a priority, where love and passion was the centerpiece, and it all happened...at the right time.

More Stories by Delaney Diamond

Hot Latin Men series
The Arrangement
Fight for Love
Private Acts
The Ultimate Merger
Second Chances
More Than a Mistress (coming soon)
Hot Latin Men: Vol. I (print anthology)
Hot Latin Men: Vol. II (print anthology)

Hawthorne Family series
The Temptation of a Good Man
A Hard Man to Love
Here Comes Trouble
For Better or Worse
Hawthorne Family Series: Vol. I (print anthology)
Hawthorne Family Series: Vol. II (print anthology)

Love Unexpected series
The Blind Date
The Wrong Man
An Unexpected Attraction
The Right Time

Johnson Family series
Unforgettable
Perfect
Just Friends
The Rules
Good Behavior (coming soon)

Bailar series (sweet/clean romance)
Worth Waiting For

Stand Alones
Still in Love
Subordinate Position

Free Stories
www.delaneydiamond.com

About the Author

Delaney Diamond is the USA Today Bestselling Author of sweet, sensual, passionate romance novels. Originally from the U.S. Virgin Islands, she now lives in Atlanta, Georgia. She reads romance novels, mysteries, thrillers, and a fair amount of nonfiction. When she's not busy reading or writing, she's in the kitchen trying out new recipes, dining at one of her favorite restaurants, or traveling to an interesting locale. She speaks fluent conversational French and can get by in Spanish.

Enjoy free reads and the first chapter of all her novels on her website. Join her e-mail mailing list to get sneak peeks, notices of sale prices, and find out about new releases.

www.delaneydiamond.com